PRAISE FOR CHAD ZUNKER

AN EQUAL JUSTICE

"A thriller with a message. A pleasure to read. Twists I didn't see coming.
I read it in one sitting."
  —Robert Dugoni, #1 Amazon bestselling author of *My Sister's Grave*

"Taut, suspenseful, and action-packed with a hero you can root for,
Zunker has hit it out of the park with this one."
  —Victor Methos, bestselling author of *The Neon Lawyer*

"A gripping thriller with a heart, *An Equal Justice* hits the ground
running . . . The chapters flew by, with surprises aplenty and taut writing.
A highly recommended read that introduces a lawyer with legs."
  —Crime Thriller Hound

THE TRACKER

"A gritty, compelling, and altogether engrossing novel that reads as if
ripped from the headlines. I couldn't turn the pages fast enough. Chad
Zunker is the real deal."
  —Christopher Reich, *New York Times* bestselling author of
  Numbered Account and *Rules of Deception*

"*Good Will Hunting* meets *The Bourne Identity*."
  —Fred Burton, *New York Times* bestselling author of *Under Fire*

AN

UNEQUAL
DEFENSE

OTHER TITLES BY CHAD ZUNKER

DAVID ADAMS SERIES

An Equal Justice

SAM CALLAHAN SERIES

The Tracker
The Shadow Shepherd
Hunt the Lion

AN
UNEQUAL
DEFENSE

CHAD ZUNKER

Text copyright © 2020 by Chad Zunker
All rights reserved.

Published by Thomas & Mercer, Seattle

www.apub.com

Amazon, the Amazon logo, and Thomas & Mercer are trademarks of Amazon.com, Inc., or its affiliates.

ISBN-13: 9781542000055
ISBN-10: 154200005X

Cover design by Rex Bonomelli

Printed in the United States of America

To Katie, my wife, whose compassion for the vulnerable first pulled us into a world that has changed our lives for the better.
To my brothers and sisters on the streets, who are struggling to survive and to be known. I see you.

ONE

Rebel opened his eyes, blinked several times, and tried to focus. Where was he? The area in front of him was dark; the only light came from a lamppost down the alleyway. A few feet ahead sat two dingy metal dumpsters stuffed full of boxes and trash bags. Beneath him was cold and dirty concrete—which was not unusual. As a thirty-seven-year-old drifter who'd lived on the streets for the past five years, Rebel was used to finding himself sitting on concrete with his back pressed against the brick of a random building.

He felt disoriented. Had he had a spell?

Putting a hand on his head, Rebel noticed he was wearing a knit cap. That didn't make any sense to him. He never wore hats of any kind. He yanked it off, stared at it, confused. A black ski cap? Where had he gotten it? Then his eyes drifted down to his chest, where he discovered he was also wearing an army-green jacket. It had some kind of unfamiliar military stitching on the front left breast pocket. This was not his jacket, either. Had he taken it from someone?

Pushing himself up off the concrete, Rebel squinted, peered down the alley in both directions. He noticed two men sleeping on top of cardboard boxes in another doorway of the same building ten feet over from him. They were wrapped in dirty blankets, and both looked asleep—or passed out. Rebel thought he recognized the older guy with the scraggly gray beard but couldn't place his name at the moment. Turning around, Rebel could hear rock music pumping from inside the building behind him.

Was he back in Moscow? How long had he been there?

He put both of his hands in the front pockets of the green jacket, searching for answers. His left hand came up empty. But his right hand gripped a familiar metal object. What the hell?

He pulled out a gun, his eyes shooting wide-open. Startled, he flexed his fingers involuntarily, squeezing the trigger, suddenly setting the gun off. A loud gunshot rang out, a bullet ricocheting off the concrete just inches from his foot, scaring the hell out of him.

Rebel stared at the gun in his shaky hand. Why did he have a gun? He hated guns and never used them anymore. Not since he'd bolted from the program.

Glancing over to his left, Rebel made out a guy lying facedown on the concrete in the middle of the alley about twenty feet from him. The man wasn't moving. He wore a white button-down, slacks, nice black dress shoes. There was something familiar about him. Then Rebel noticed smoke lingering in the air a few feet to the left of the man—like someone had just exhaled a puff from a cigarette. Beneath the smoke, Rebel spotted a face staring right at him from another back doorway of the building.

Rebel felt a charge go through him. Was the guy a Russian agent? Had they finally found him? The guy in the doorway stepped out a bit, a pool of light now washing over his face. He didn't look like Russian intelligence. Was he CIA? A phone was pressed to his ear. Was he calling for backup? Were more spooks about to be all over the alley?

Rebel cursed, felt his heart racing. Getting taken in by the CIA might be worse for him than being captured by the Russians. He had to get the hell out of there right now before it was too late. He could never let the CIA take him back to the dragon's lair.

TWO

David Adams was startled awake when a light popped on down the office hallway. It took him a moment to clear the fog from his brain. What time was it? He knew it was past midnight, since that was around the time he'd finally dozed off. Sitting up from the cheap sofa, David pulled earplugs from his ears—something he wore each night to block out the noise from the Speakeasy, a 1920s-style cocktail bar next door that shared rickety walls with his run-down office building. He could still hear the music pumping, which meant it was not yet two in the morning, when the place finally closed down for the night. The law firm he'd started with Thomas Gray, his mentor, leased a tiny office space on the second floor of a three-story redbrick building that just happened to sit directly across the street from his former legal home—the pristine Frost Bank Tower, with all its shiny glass, metal, and steel.

He rubbed his eyes, glanced around the back room. There was an old wooden desk shoved into one corner, a cheap fold-out table that held a coffee maker against a side wall, a mini fridge beside it, and a metal bookcase loaded down with stacks of legal books. The back room was their library, kitchen, *and* lounge, all rolled into one cramped space. Lately, the back room had also doubled as David's bedroom. Thomas knew he'd been sleeping at the office lately to save money on rent—a clear violation of their lease agreement. But David had insisted it would be only until he could find a more affordable living situation. That was eight weeks ago. David had been showering and getting dressed at the Gold's Gym around the corner most mornings before work. He was grateful for the reasonable thirty-nine-dollar-a-month membership. In many ways, he was now living only a few short rungs up the ladder from his clients these days.

A noise came from the entry room. Was he being robbed? He felt certain he'd locked the office, so the only way inside was with a key—or someone breaking and entering. That was always a possibility with the type of clients he now represented. He found he could be their best friend one moment, their worst enemy the next. It just came with the territory as a street lawyer. David had been learning that the hard way the past six months, ever since he'd walked out the golden doors of Hunter & Kellerman, the richest law firm in Austin, to help form Gray & Adams, LLP.

David's clients were no longer billion-dollar tech companies who promptly paid his $475-per-hour associate rate to shuffle around a mind-numbing amount of nonsensical paperwork. His client list had been swiftly replaced by a growing group of ragtag characters who wore dirty, mismatched clothes and spent most nights in shelters or alleys, under bridges, or in the woods. Most of his new friends could barely pay him a dime—if that. Which was why David had given up his luxury condo a few blocks away and had been sleeping on this stiff sofa the past couple of months.

Another bang in the entry room. Someone was definitely out there. Thomas? David reached into the sofa cushions for his cell phone. No missed calls or texts from his partner. Standing, he grabbed a wooden baseball bat leaning against the wall next to the mini fridge—one that he sometimes swung around a bit to help him think better. David stepped cautiously down the hallway, wearing only a gray Stanford Law

T-shirt and blue boxer shorts. Whoever was in the entry room—a space that doubled as their conference room—made no attempt to be quiet.

David was damn near ready to take a swing when he spotted a friendly face sitting at the round table, eating a sandwich from a white sack.

"Doc?" David said. "What the hell? I almost clubbed you."

"Sorry to wake you, Shep," Doc said. "But we need to talk."

David dropped the bat to his side, his shoulders relaxing. Everyone on the streets called him Shep, the nickname a homeless street preacher named Benny had given him last year before the old man had tragically died.

"It's the middle of the night," David stated.

"It's important."

"You okay?"

"Yeah, I'm fine," Doc assured him. "But someone else is in big trouble."

"All right, gimme a second. Let me at least get my pants on."

Doc was a tall, slender man in his late fifties with salt-and-pepper hair. David had first met him last summer when Benny had walked David deep into the woods for his first visit to the Camp—a secret tent community for a group of homeless men. Doc had been one of the founders of the Camp before it had burned to the ground last year. After partnering with Thomas, David had hired Doc to do part-time legal research for him. Turned out the man was one hell of a paralegal. Doc had taught high school history for a lot of years down near Galveston before he spiraled into alcoholism, separated from his family, then fell into his long bout with homelessness.

After putting on his jeans, David returned to the front room.

"What is it?" David asked. "Who's in trouble?"

"You know Rebel?"

David pondered the name, shook his head.

"You've probably seen him around town," Doc said. "A bit of a hell-raiser but harmless, if you ask me."

"Okay. What about him?"

"He got arrested a couple of hours ago."

"For what?"

"Murder."

David felt his shoulders tense up again. He wasn't used to hearing the word *murder* associated with any of his street associates. Most of their legal troubles revolved around topics like petty theft, being drunk and disorderly, and disturbing the peace.

David pulled out a second chair, sat across from Doc. "Who did he kill?"

"He's being *accused* of killing a county prosecutor earlier tonight in an alley near Sixth and Trinity."

David felt the tension now race up to his neck. A prosecutor? He'd expected Doc to say Rebel had killed another homeless guy. Not an attorney. David had gotten to know quite a few prosecutors over the past few months. He also had two good friends and former Stanford classmates who worked inside the DA's office—which gave him sudden pause.

"Do you know the name of the prosecutor?" David asked.

"A guy named Luke Murphy is what they're saying."

"No," David gasped, feeling a hard punch to the gut. He slumped in his chair as a sudden wave of emotion pressed in on him and took his breath away. Murphy had grown up in small-town West Texas, like David, which was how they'd first connected while at Stanford. David also knew Murphy's wife, Michelle, who had worked full-time as a middle school teacher back in Palo Alto while her husband had finished law school. The Murphys had two small children, a boy and a girl, and David couldn't imagine the feeling of devastation inside that household right now.

"I guess you know him?" Doc asked.

David nodded. "What happened?"

"They say Rebel shot him."

"Are you suggesting you don't believe Rebel actually did it?"

Doc shook his head. "It's hard for me to see it. I mean, the man's a bit of a wild card and certainly a crazy talker—constantly spouting off these conspiracies about men who he says are always out to get him, telling us about all these dangerous fights he's been involved in over the years—but I just have a difficult time believing he'd do something like *this*."

"Are there any witnesses?"

"I haven't been able to confirm anything yet. It's not like the cops will talk to me. I was hoping you might get involved."

"Involved how?"

"He'll need a lawyer."

David tilted his head. "You want me to represent the guy?"

"I just want you to go talk to him. Get the truth."

"No way. The truth is, I don't want any part of this. Luke Murphy was my friend. I know his wife and kids. And we're talking about a case where the victim is a county prosecutor, not just some guy off the street. Whoever stupidly takes this on will feel the full weight of the DA's office. Not to mention when the media finds out, this will probably be a three-ring circus."

"The media already has it," Doc said.

David walked into his front office, which had a view over Congress Avenue, and flipped on the small TV he had set up on a credenza against the wall. He switched channels from ESPN to a local twenty-four-hour news channel. He immediately saw a photo of Luke Murphy on the screen, with his full head of dark hair and strong jaw, the words Assistant District Attorney Shot Dead in big bold letters at the bottom, sending another jolt through him. The female reporter said Murphy had been with the DA's office for the past two years and was respected by all. The screen then cut away to police cars surrounding the corner of Sixth and Trinity. The reporter mentioned the police already had a suspect in custody, but the identity had not yet been released.

"What do you think?" Doc asked, watching the TV from behind David.

"Sorry, Doc, but I don't want to touch this thing with a ten-foot pole."

"You should know something first before you make that decision."

"What?"

"Benny and Rebel were friends."

David turned to Doc with a wrinkled brow.

Doc explained. "Benny brought Rebel out to the Camp two years ago. While most guys on the streets steered clear of Rebel, Benny moved in even closer."

"That does not surprise me."

"Yeah, well, Benny really got to know Rebel and began to peel away at his hard outer layer. I'll admit I was skeptical because of Rebel's erratic behavior, but I really started to believe Benny might make a breakthrough with him. You could tell Rebel was starting to embrace our community at the Camp."

"So what happened?" David had not met the man during his visit to the Camp last year.

Doc sighed, shrugged. "Too many strange voices in the man's head, I think. Rebel just upped and vanished one night, and we didn't see him again for more than six months. When he finally showed back up in Austin, he seemed even worse off than before. More paranoid, more frantic. Benny tried again but just couldn't get anywhere with him. But he never stopped trying. You know Benny; he would never give up on people. All the way up to the day Benny died, he still believed Rebel could be saved."

David thought about that for a moment. Benny had meant the world to him. The old man had entered his life last year like a divine tornado and had turned everything upside down in a meaningful way.

If Benny had once tried to save Rebel, shouldn't he at least go talk to the guy? Did he owe the old man that much?

"Damn it, Doc." He sighed. "Maybe you should be the lawyer and not me. You sure as hell know how to make your case."

"You'll go talk to him?"

"I'll go talk to him, but that's all."

THREE

After slipping on his brown leather jacket and running shoes, David walked the four blocks from his office building over to the chaotic crime scene at the corner of Sixth and Trinity. He wanted to get a look for himself before heading to the county jail to talk to Rebel. A half dozen police cars were parked up and down the street, along with other emergency vehicles, red-and-blue lights still flashing, barricades up everywhere. Since the shooting had occurred near the city's popular bar-and-entertainment district, a big crowd of people had gathered around the perimeter. Most looked like drunk fraternity guys who just wanted to get on TV. Several reporters with cameras seemed happy to oblige, shoving microphones in faces, while overzealous buddies hooted and hollered behind them like they were at a sporting event.

Weaving through the crowd, David sidled up to a uniformed police officer who was standing off by himself near a barricade.

"What happened?" David asked.

The officer turned to him. "Some homeless guy killed a county prosecutor tonight."

"How?"

"Shot him in the head in that alley."

"Damn."

David glanced a half block down the street, away from the crowd, spotted Murphy's white Ford Escape parked along the curb of Trinity Street. The faded TCU sticker was still in place on the car's bumper like it had been all throughout law school. The crime scene did not currently include the vehicle. Maybe no one knew it belonged to Murphy. What had his friend been doing here tonight?

Seeing the vehicle made David think of Jen Cantwell, his ex-girlfriend, who drove the same model car. A month after David had said his final goodbye to Hunter & Kellerman, Jen had returned home to Virginia to take care of her suddenly ailing mother. It was an excruciating goodbye for both of them, knowing there was no clear timeline for her to return—if ever. Jen had already landed a meaningful job with a nonprofit there and had quickly settled into a new life. They had done a month of phone calls and texts before they both decided it was too damn difficult to stay connected. Even though they'd dated only a short time, he'd fallen fast and hard. Jen was the only woman with whom he'd ever been completely vulnerable. The past five months had been a serious uphill battle. He had not expected to start his new life without her.

David looked back over toward the crime scene.

"Any idea what a prosecutor was doing in that alley?" he asked the officer.

"Hell if I know," the officer replied. "Getting himself shot."

David slipped behind the crowd of onlookers. It was difficult to imagine Murphy being shot and killed in that alley just a few hours ago. One moment here; the next moment gone. What really happened? He thought of his good-natured friend, who was always cracking redneck jokes at his own expense—most of which their elitist law school classmates never understood. It had been several months since they'd last hung out; both of them were so busy. Murphy had seemed happy with his work in the DA's office and pleased with the life he and Michelle had made for themselves in Austin. Now all that was over. Michelle must be crushed. At the right time, David would pay his condolences.

David took in the scene again, felt an uneasiness begin to swell in the pit of his stomach. He suddenly realized that tonight's tragedy had happened in the same dark alley where Benny had been murdered last year. Two of his good friends both gunned down near the exact same spot in a big city.

Coincidence? Or fate?

It was time for him to go talk to Rebel.

FOUR

David found several TV reporters stationed outside the criminal justice complex, cameras rolling, bright lights blaring in their faces. He made sure to discreetly slip inside the county jail entrance, as he certainly didn't want any of them trying to shove a microphone in front of him right now and start asking questions. He had nothing to say at this point. He still didn't know what he was doing there. After passing through security, he checked in with Lolita, a familiar face who sat behind the front desk's glass partition. In her twenties, Lolita had curly black hair and a snarky attitude and usually worked the late shift. David had been a regular visitor to the jail during late-night hours since a lot of his clients chose to do dumb things in the middle of the night.

"You sure you want this one, honey?" Lolita asked him, shaking her head. "Those reporters aren't out there at this hour for kicks. And from what I've been hearing in the hallways behind me, this guy's a real nut job. He's been bouncing off the walls, talking about alien abductions and other nonsense. I wouldn't go near it, if I were you."

"I just want to talk to him as a favor to someone else."

"All right. It's your neck."

"Can you get me a private room?"

She frowned at him. "You his lawyer?"

"Not yet."

"Well, when you're officially his lawyer, you can get whatever you need through the proper channels. I have to be extra careful with this one."

David leaned in, whispered, "Come on, Lolita. You owe me."

She sighed, frowned. "Give me a second."

David stopped her. "Hey, one more small thing . . ."

She glared at him. "What?"

"Can you also get me a copy of the arrest affidavit?"

"Damn it, David."

She stepped away from the front desk. David had helped Lolita's nineteen-year-old cousin get probation for a parole violation a few months ago. David had been using it to leverage little favors here and there around the jail.

Turning around, he noticed one of the male reporters standing right outside the glass doors of the jail and trying to peer inside. David quickly spun back around. The jail's small lobby was nearly empty at this hour, so his sudden presence inside was likely drawing some attention. They probably suspected he was a lawyer. When he was done talking with Rebel, David planned to escape out a back exit.

Lolita finally sauntered back up to the front desk and discreetly handed him a folded sheet of paper—a copy of the officer's written statement for probable cause in the arrest of Roger Eugene North.

"You're the best," he told Lolita.

"You didn't get that from me."

"Right."

"I let the boys know you're out here," she said. "Told them you *may* or *may not* be the crazy guy's lawyer, so not sure what that'll get you as far as any urgency. You'd better get comfortable waiting."

Sitting in the small lobby as far from the front windows as possible, David quickly read over the officer's brief arrest statement. There wasn't much to it, which was normal with these reports. At approximately ten thirty, police had received a 911 call from a man named Brad Shaw, who identified himself as an employee at Burnside's Tavern on Sixth Street. Shaw stated he was taking a smoke break when he found a man who looked to be shot dead in the alley directly behind the bar's back door. Moments later, Shaw said he heard a gunshot in the alley, maybe twenty feet away. He then spotted a man wearing a green jacket and a black hat toss something into a dumpster and run the opposite way out of the alley. Officers promptly responded and found the suspect on the sidewalk a few blocks away. The suspect tried to flee and appeared to be in some kind of drug-induced rage. He spoke in a rapid and incoherent fashion and had to be restrained by three officers. The gun believed to be used in the killing, which the suspect admitted to firing, was recovered from the alley dumpster a few minutes later. Shaw, the witness, then confirmed the suspect was the same man he'd spotted in the alley, at which point the suspect was booked.

David sat back, pondered the written statement. By all indications, it sure as hell looked like Rebel had shot and killed Luke Murphy. Why?

David waited nearly an hour before a deputy finally pushed open an ugly blue door to the back and called out for him. He was then led down a long hallway, where the deputy opened the door to a private room with a small table and two chairs.

"You sure you want to be alone with this guy?" the deputy asked him.

"Is he that unstable?"

"Yep. Let's keep him cuffed."

"All right."

The deputy disappeared down the hallway. David paced in a tight circle around the room. Thinking of Michelle Murphy, a brand-new widow, he felt really uneasy. What would she think about him sitting down with the man who had just shot and killed her husband? Two minutes later, the deputy arrived with Rebel in tow, hands cuffed in front, ankles shackled, wearing the same standard black-and-gray-striped jail jumpsuit that David had seen on several other clients over the past few months.

Rebel was thirty-seven, according to the arrest affidavit, and had a full head of reddish-brown hair that flowed down to his shoulders, along with a thick mustache that would give Tom Selleck a run for his money. David's first thought was that Rebel had a movie-star look about him. Nice hair, clear blue eyes, strong jaw, and a ruggedly handsome face, though a bit weathered. Standing around six feet, Rebel seemed lean and muscular under the jumpsuit. He did not have the gaunt and shaggy appearance of so many others who lived out on the streets full-time. He was not at all what David had envisioned.

The deputy made Rebel sit in the chair across the table from where David stood.

"Don't give us any trouble," the deputy warned Rebel, before telling David he'd be right outside if the inmate tried anything stupid.

David nodded, waited for the deputy to shut the door. He then turned his attention to Rebel, who'd had his narrow eyes set on David from the moment he first entered the private room.

"You one of them?" Rebel immediately asked.

"Who? The police?"

"Nah, man," Rebel scoffed. "I ain't worried about the police."

"Why not?"

"Police can't touch me. I'm a free bird, and they're clueless. Now answer my question. You one of them?"

"I don't know to whom you're referring."

"CIA," Rebel hissed through clenched teeth.

David sat in the chair opposite the table from Rebel. "No, I'm not with the CIA. My name is David Adams—"

"You Russian intelligence?" Rebel interrupted him. "You do have the look of a Commie. You damn Russians been trying to take me out for years."

"Why's that?" David asked, not yet sure how to navigate this early exchange. He was already being fed a heavy dose of the conspiracy-theory nonsense Doc had mentioned earlier. He thought it might be good to let it play out some so he had a better idea of how Rebel's mind worked.

Rebel smiled wide, showing incredibly straight teeth. "I know *everything*."

"About . . . ?"

Another small grin and shrug. "About Russia's infiltration of America. Commie agents everywhere. A list that could fill up a damn phone book. I've seen it with my own eyes." He glanced at the door, leaned forward on the table, lowered his voice. "I know who really found Osama bin Laden. Believe me, the news folks got it all wrong. Did you know the CIA paid two hundred million to get us credit for it?"

"Paid who?"

Rebel's eyes narrowed. "Don't try your tricks with me, Commie. It won't work. I've seen them all. I'm a cowboy."

David tried to hide his dismay over how far gone the man seemed to be right now. "I'm a lawyer, not Russian intelligence."

"A lawyer?" Rebel eased back a touch. "What the hell do you want, Lawyer? My money? I ain't giving you no money, I can tell you that for damn sure."

"I don't want your money. Do you understand why you're in jail tonight?"

"Do I look stupid to you, Lawyer? They say I shot a man."

Rebel didn't expound, as if it were no big deal.

"And . . . ?" David asked.

"And what, Lawyer? Haven't you been listening? It's all a big setup. The CIA wants to drag me back to the dragon's lair. But I ain't going. Mark that down, you hear me? They might as well strap me in the chair and stick me with that deadly poison right now. Because I ain't *never* going back there again. You know what they do to people in that place?"

David was afraid to even ask about the dragon's lair. "Can we talk about tonight? And what happened?"

Rebel ignored him. "It ain't just regular people they got locked up over there, either." He lowered his voice to a whisper. "They also got aliens hidden there that they torture for information. I've seen them creatures with my own eyes. Been having nightmares about them for years."

"Did you shoot the man in the alley tonight?" David asked directly, trying to steer the conversation back to reality.

Again, Rebel didn't answer him. "Why should I even talk to you, Lawyer? Every lawyer I ever knew was out to screw me. Either working for the government, or trying to go after my money. Was a stupid lawyer that turned my wife on me, made her think I was crazy. I should've shot him, I tell you what."

"Look, Rebel, I'm here trying to help, okay?"

The man leaned forward, cuffed hands on the table, voice again at a whisper. "How the hell do you know my name?"

David guessed no one inside the jail facility tonight was calling him *Rebel*. That was his street name—it wasn't in his file. He hoped it might be an entryway toward a more normal conversation, if that was even possible.

"Benny was a good friend of mine," David explained.

Rebel's eyes remained locked on him. But he didn't say a word.

"I heard you two were also friends," David added.

"Who told you that?"

"Doc. That's why I'm here. Doc asked me to come see you."

The mention of both Benny and Doc seemed to snap Rebel out of whatever conspiracy fog had been controlling his mind. David could practically see the hard edge around his eyes begin to soften, as if a switch had suddenly flipped. The man's whole face relaxed.

"Doc is good people," Rebel offered, nodding, easing back.

"I agree," David replied. "So was Benny."

Rebel stared off into the corner of the room, an easy grin gradually covering the length of his tan face, as if he were thinking about better days. "Benny always made me laugh. Everyone tries to say I'm crazy, but, nah, man, Benny was the crazy one. While we're all out there saving ourselves, Benny was trying to save us, one by one, with all that God talk. Not sure I believe any of it, but I liked some of what he had to say. Heaven. Grace. I liked listening to him, too. Doesn't seem right that he's gone. Benny always treated me fair. I wasn't always the best to him. I regret that now."

"Benny was a forgiving kind of man."

Rebel's eyes shifted back over to David. "You were Benny's lawyer? The one I heard about?"

"I'm not sure what all you've heard, but, yes, I was Benny's lawyer."

"Now you want to be my lawyer?"

"I don't know yet."

Rebel pulled his cuffed hands back into his lap, seemed to relax even more. It was almost as if David were looking at a completely different person. "I didn't shoot anyone tonight, Lawyer."

David leaned forward. "Then tell me what happened."

Rebel shrugged. "Not really sure. I had a spell. Don't remember much."

"A spell?"

"Been happening for years, ever since I escaped the dragon's lair. They messed me up real bad inside there. Everything just goes dark for a while, here and there. I lose track of things."

"You're saying you blacked out tonight?"

He nodded. "Woke up in that alley. Not even sure how I got there. I was wearing a jacket and a black hat I didn't even recognize. Found a gun in the pocket of the jacket. Startled me, and I accidentally fired that damn thing off. The sound of that gun going off scared the hell out of me, so I took off running. Next thing I know, I'm being tackled by a couple of goons in uniforms."

"What did you do with the gun?"

"Tossed it. I don't need a gun. I can handle myself just fine."

"Police are saying that gun was used to kill a man in that same alley only a few minutes before a witness saw you throw it in the dumpster."

"I know what they're saying, Lawyer," Rebel replied, calm and measured. "Couple of meathead detectives damn near shouted it at me for over two hours trying to get me to straight-up confess."

"What did you tell them?"

"Same thing I'm telling you. I didn't shoot anyone."

David sat back. "These blackouts. How long do they usually last?"

He shrugged. "Sometimes a few minutes. Sometimes a half hour."

"And you don't recall where you were or what you were doing right before you had this spell tonight?"

He shook his head. "Nope."

"Is it normal for you to not remember what happened before a blackout?"

He shrugged again. "Ain't nothing normal about me, Lawyer."

"Did you know Luke Murphy?" David asked, trying a redirect. He watched Rebel carefully, wanting to gauge his response to the victim's name.

"Who?"

"The man who was killed in the alley tonight."

"Like I told the cops, I don't know that name. Means nothing to me."

"How do you think you got that gun, Rebel?"

"No clue."

"Are you trying to convince me that someone planted it on you while you were blacked out?"

"I ain't trying to convince you of nothing."

"Well, you have to admit it all sounds a bit far-fetched."

David's response seemed to flip the same switch again in the man's brain, taking him right back to frantic conspiracy land. Rebel's eyes went from soft to hard in a split second. "I've been telling you already, Lawyer, it's the damn CIA. Why the hell ain't you listening?" He quickly grew even more agitated. "They the ones that must've planted that gun on me! This is all a big setup so I won't tell the whole world what I know about them!"

"Calm down a sec, Rebel," David urged him, trying to get hold of the situation again. But it was too late. The man was already off the rails.

Rebel suddenly stood, sending his metal chair flying back and banging hard against the room's outer wall. Then he started yelling even louder. "Hell, Lawyer, the Russians could be working *with* the CIA on this one, I tell you! They want to take me back to the dragon's lair, but I sure as hell won't go without a fight!"

The door to the private room swung open, two deputies rushing inside at the sound of all the yelling and banging. One deputy grabbed Rebel around the shoulders. Rebel tried to thrust himself loose again as the second deputy clutched him around the neck, both deputies working hard to subdue him.

"It's the CIA, Lawyer!" Rebel yelled.

David stood, not sure what to make of this. As they dragged Rebel from the room, he kept pleading with David.

"Please don't let them send me back to the dragon's lair!"

FIVE

Early the next morning, David sprinted through the streets of downtown in his business suit, briefcase in hand, tie flapping over his shoulder, while sweat poured down his face. His twenty-two-year-old client, Bill Hadley—known as Billy the Kid on the streets—had a court appearance for his third public intoxication arrest in the past twelve months. David was running late because his beat-up old truck wouldn't start this morning. The fifteen-year-old Chevy that had replaced his beloved Range Rover Sport had been barely stuttering to a start for a few weeks now. While a desperate prayer had worked the past couple of days—the tired engine would eventually turn over for him—David had no such luck today. The truck was completely dead. And so was David's relationship with Judge Henry if he didn't make it on time to the Downtown Austin Community Court. Judge Henry had already reprimanded him several times for being late to his courtroom.

A wave of body odor slapped David in the face as he entered a nondescript court building that sat at the east edge of the popular bar district. Most of those who passed through this court day in and day out lived on the streets full-time.

After breezing through a security checkpoint, David paused before entering Judge Henry's courtroom. He wiped sweat from his brow onto his black suit sleeve, took a few deep breaths, tried to slow down his racing heart rate and gather himself, then pushed through the doors. His client was already standing behind the defense table, looking helpless. The prosecutor, a decent guy named Larry Wilkerson, turned, shook his head, and smiled at David.

"Well, look who finally decided to show up," Judge Henry said, peering at him over his reading glasses from up front. "Have we not already discussed your tardiness in my courtroom, Mr. Adams?"

In his sixties with gray hair, Judge Henry was an intimidating character. At six-nine, he had once played basketball at Texas Tech. So when he stood up behind the bench, he towered over everyone. Thankfully, he was still sitting, which led David to believe he wasn't altogether too pissed. At least, David hoped he wasn't.

David hustled to the front, dropped his briefcase to the floor. "Yes, sir, and I apologize once again, Judge. It won't happen again."

Judge Henry frowned. But then again, he was always frowning. "I think I'll help you remember for next time, Counselor. Court fines you two hundred dollars."

"Seriously?" David snapped. He was only four minutes late.

"Do I look like a comedian, Mr. Adams? And if it does happen again, it'll go up to five hundred. Are we clear, son?"

"Yes, Your Honor," David said.

Cursing under his breath, David realized he'd now make *nothing* on this case. Not a single dollar. Although Billy had agreed to scrounge up $200 for David to handle this legal matter, the court fine today made this a complete wash.

"Good. Let's finally get started."

David turned to look at his client, who was damn near skin and bones with spiky yellow hair and a small patch of brown hair under his chin. Billy had at least managed to find a decent brown button-down shirt to wear along with his dirty blue jeans. The shirt was tucked into his pants, like David had requested. His client also wore the dark blue tie David had let him borrow—although the knot at the top was completely botched.

"Where the hell you been, Shep?" Billy whispered.

"Car trouble," David said.

"Geez. Almost peed my pants standing here."

David noticed Billy's eyes were bloodshot. And he could smell alcohol all over the man's breath. Unbelievable. His client was making a court appearance for his third public intoxication charge—after Billy the Kid had cursed out a police officer and gotten himself arrested outside a restaurant—and the idiot was actually showing up to court drunk? Billy seemed to recognize the disturbed look on David's face.

"Sorry, Shep," he muttered. "I was just *so* nervous today."

"Don't say a word to *anyone*," David ordered through clenched teeth.

Billy swallowed, nodded.

Wilkerson was asking the judge for thirty days' jail time.

Judge Henry looked over to David. "I'm inclined to agree, Mr. Adams. Your client doesn't seem to be learning his lesson."

"I understand that position, Your Honor," David said. "But my client has a three-year-old son whom he helps provide for each week through various part-time work. Any jail time for him could seriously hinder the mother's ability to properly care for and feed the boy."

Judge Henry shifted his attention to Billy. "This true, Mr. Hadley?"

Billy didn't answer. He just stood there, wide-eyed.

The judge looked annoyed. "Mr. Hadley, I'm speaking to you."

David turned to his client, gave him a "What the hell are you doing?" look.

"You said don't talk," Billy whispered, barely moving his lips.

"What's going on, Mr. Adams?" the judge asked, his irritation growing.

"Answer the judge," David told Billy as calmly as he could.

Billy looked up at the bench. "Uh, yessir, Judge Harry," he began, butchering Judge Henry's name. "I do gotta boy. Stays with his mom. Name is Nick, but I call him Nitro—he's a fast little booger, you see. Always running circles around me. Not sure how it all happened, Judge, especially because his mom ain't much to look at and all. But, you see, it gets lonely out there on the streets, and—"

David raised his hand to cut off his client. Not only was Billy going off on a disturbing tangent, his words were beginning to slur. David could sense Judge Henry's pensive eyes on his client. The judge was probably beginning to wonder whether Billy was the usual courtroom wacko—or something else. David needed to take things in another direction before the judge's curiosity grew, or else Billy could come out of this with way more than thirty days in jail.

"Judge, I'd like to ask for one hundred eighty days of probation. My client will also agree to perform twenty hours of community service and attend treatment classes for alcohol addiction. But you can't take food out of a child's mouth, Your Honor. The mother is not working—she has physical disabilities—so she is barely making it. If my client goes to jail, the mother falls off the deep end, and Nicholas probably ends up lost in the system somewhere. I think we can all agree that's not the best thing for that boy."

Although David thought jail time might be good for Billy—maybe his client would finally take all this more seriously—everything he'd just told the judge about caring for the boy was true. His client might be a class A moron, but Billy did somehow manage to wrangle up a few bucks every week that he gave to the boy's mother. David thought that was an honorable thing to do, especially when it forced his client to sleep most nights in a crowded room next to a hundred other desperate men over at the ARCH, the Austin Resource Center for the Homeless.

"Fine," Judge Henry said. "I agree the boy needs to be with his mother. But I'm going to hold you personally accountable, Mr. Adams, if your client doesn't attend every single one of those classes. Agreed?"

"Yes, Your Honor."

"Don't forget to pay the court fine on your way out," Judge Henry added, before moving on to the next legal matter.

David took Billy by the arm, eager to escort him out of the building before anyone else noticed the alcohol stench. After paying his fine, David huddled with his client across the street.

"Thank you so much," Billy kept saying to him. "I owe you big-time, man. You're the best. That judge can be a real hard-ass."

"The only thing you owe me is our agreed-upon legal fee. So pay up."

"Yeah, okay," Billy said, reaching down into his pocket. But he had a certain look on his face that concerned David. Like a teenager who'd just been busted by his father for sneaking out in the car. Billy pulled out a wad of wrinkled cash, handed it to David, who quickly counted it out.

"This is only eighteen dollars," David said. "You were supposed to have *two hundred* for me by today, Billy. That was our agreement."

"I know, I know. I'm real sorry. I just don't got it today."

"Why not? You said you got that job over at the car wash."

"Well, you see, there was this tricycle thing for Nitro. Cost me fifty dollars, man. But I had to get it for him. You should've seen his face—"

David interrupted. "What about the rest of the money?"

Another guilty look spread over his client's face. "I'm an idiot, Shep. I always say I'm just gonna have one drink, and before I know it, I've spent damn near everything in my pockets. I gotta take those classes, just like the judge said, you know. Get my life together."

David sighed. "Yes, I do know. And, believe me, you will be attending every single one of those classes, or I'll probably end up fined by the court again. And I can't afford that. So don't go hiding somewhere I can't find you."

"I won't. I swear. And I'll get you the money, I promise."

They parted ways. Standing there, David shook his head. How many times had he heard that kind of empty promise from a client over the past six months? Too many to count. With the court fine, David calculated he'd just *lost* $182 on this case.

Which was about par for the course these days.

David met Thomas for breakfast at 1886 Café & Bakery, a few blocks up the street from their office. Lately, they'd been forced to regularly meet outside the office if they wanted to discuss any real law firm business. David's growing client list had made their office a popular hangout for the downtown transients who wanted a brief escape from the heat, the cold, or just the mind-numbing boredom of living out on the streets. There seemed to always be at least one or two guys sitting around in the front room, eating their extra food, talking too loudly, hoping to strike up random conversations with anyone who passed their way—seemingly oblivious to the fact that both David and Thomas were actual lawyers who had real work to do.

Most of them were harmless. There were a couple of guys who were a bit rough around the edges. The oddest was a black man in his seventies who had a prominent white beard, called himself Bobby E. Lee, and wore a full-on gray Confederate soldier uniform every day. David still wasn't sure what to make of the paradox since the old man didn't say much at all. He'd just show up at the office most days, pull a chair right outside the front door of their suite, sit quietly, and act as if he were guarding a military fort. The rich lawyers over at Hunter & Kellerman weren't the only ones with a heightened security presence. No one got past Bobby Lee unnoticed.

"You look like hell," Thomas said to David, sipping his coffee.

"Didn't sleep well."

"It would probably help if you slept on a real bed and not a crappy sofa."

"I'm working on that."

27

"I keep telling you that you can use our guest bedroom. Lori doesn't mind."

"And I keep telling you, no, but thanks."

"You really are a stubborn ass."

They shared a grin. A slender man in his midthirties with short blond hair, Thomas had been a refuge for David in the aftermath of his dramatic departure from H&K last year. His partner was married to a terrific woman, who constantly stocked their office's mini fridge with delicious homemade food. They had two young daughters. David trusted no one more than Thomas.

A waitress came by and took their orders. David glanced out the window. The shooting of Luke Murphy had happened only a couple of blocks away. David had spent most of the previous night tossing and turning. He couldn't stop thinking about Murphy and the tragedy that had been brought on to his family while also reliving every bizarre detail of his sit-down with Rebel inside the county jail. CIA? Russians? Aliens? The guy certainly had a lot going on in his mind. David wondered what had triggered all of it. It was clear that Rebel drifted in and out of reality. However, there had been something genuine in the man's eyes during the brief window of seminormalcy that made David want to believe him—that someone else instead of Rebel could have killed Murphy. But wanting to believe someone was innocent was a million miles away from agreeing to represent them in the court of law.

So far, every detail of what David had gathered about Murphy's death pointed straight at Rebel. The man was standing there, holding the gun, twenty feet away, just minutes after Murphy was shot dead. Even Rebel had admitted to that fact. A claim of innocence could come only from Rebel's delusional mind. David felt like he should probably just walk away from all this. Did he really want the media attention that would undoubtedly come from representing a crazy man? Did he really want Lisa Murphy to somehow think he was betraying his friendship with her husband? Not to mention a case like this would be expensive, and he doubted Rebel could pay him anything. David would lose on all fronts.

Yet every time he felt like he'd come to the wise decision to bolt, David thought of how Benny had gone to incredible lengths to try to help Rebel. And now David had been thrust into a similar position, almost as if Benny had pulled all this together from beyond the grave. If Rebel was guilty, whether the man realized it or not, he needed an attorney who would walk with him through the difficult legal process of being charged and incarcerated. Rebel needed someone who would fight for a plea deal that included getting him serious psychological help. But would Rebel even talk to another attorney? The man had refused to talk to David until he'd mentioned his connection to Benny and Doc. Turning Rebel over to an assigned public defender right now felt like feeding him directly to the wolves.

David turned back to the table when Thomas asked him a question. "You put the sign up yet at the village?"

David nodded. "Yesterday. Another small step."

"Small but meaningful."

The village was a twenty-acre property in East Austin that David had purchased at the tail end of his tenure at Hunter & Kellerman. Benny's dream had been to create his own community on the property for all the boys from the Camp—along with others who were barely surviving out on the streets of Austin. A place of their own where they would no longer be unwanted squatters. A safe spot to heal and be restored. David still had the piece of crumpled paper where Benny had sketched out a community map. The old man had shared it with him just days before his death. Benny had planned to build tiny homes with real roofs, walls, and beds. He had plans to put up a shared bathhouse with private stalls. To plant a garden with fresh vegetables. To construct a building with a real kitchen, where the boys could regularly host parties and gatherings. A village they could all finally call home. David had a professional sign made up—BENNY'S VILLAGE—and stuck it in the ground at the front of the land.

"About all I can do right now," David said. "Until I can somehow pull more cash together and get things moving along."

"You'll get there eventually. I know you're pouring your heart into it."

"And all of my money, too."

"Yeah, we need to talk about that. I updated the firm's books this morning."

David grimaced. "How bad is it?"

Thomas sighed. "We're running on fumes."

David immediately lost his appetite. This was all his fault. He was currently on his worst streak of nonpaying clients since they'd started.

"I knew it probably wasn't looking good," he said.

"Not at all, I'm afraid." Thomas set down his coffee cup, wiped his hands on a napkin, as if it was time to have a serious talk. "Look, I know when we started this thing, we said we'd both have all the freedom in the world to pursue the type of legal work we were passionate about. And unlike at H&K, we would never let money become the driving force behind anything we do with this firm. But—"

"Some of my clients need to start paying," David interjected.

"Right. I mean, your client list is five times longer than mine, but you're only bringing in *thirteen percent* of the firm's overall income right now. And my clients aren't exactly big money, either, as you know. Something's got to give soon, or we're headed for real trouble here."

Thomas had been focused on helping families through the complex foster care and adoption system. The work was meaningful. David had seen a lot of happy tears shed inside their office from grateful parents because of it. His clients also paid their modest legal bills on time.

David leaned back in his chair. "I hear what you're saying. I have to figure out a way to manage it better since I'm getting inundated at every turn. I can barely keep up with all of the requests for help."

"You know what they're calling you?"

"Who?"

"Our street friends. Doc says everyone calls you the Lawyer."

"Is that bad? I've been called a lot worse."

"You can't be the *only* attorney they all come to when they need help, David. You have to start telling some of them no, or we won't be able to keep our doors open long enough to help *any* of them. Hell, you're already sleeping at the office because every last dollar you do earn goes either to pay Doc, to help a client who needs a new wardrobe, or toward bringing this village to life. All good things, mind you, but you can't keep it up."

"I know. You're right. I apologize for putting us in this position."

"No need to apologize. Let's just begin to work our way out of it."

David sighed. He felt horrible for Thomas. His partner had already used his own savings to give their firm a year to get on its feet. It wasn't fair for David to add more financial pressure on him. At H&K, money had been *everything*. To the firm, to the client, and certainly to him. It was the golden calf to which they all bowed. Like a vortex, the pursuit of the almighty dollar had sucked the life right out of David and had damn near taken his life off the rails. Until Benny and the boys at the Camp had rescued him. And now, ironically, money had once again become central to everything in his world—only in a polar-opposite way.

Where was the balance? While his intentions were good, David had put their firm into dire financial straits over the past six months. Had any of it really been worth it? Was he making any real difference by keeping a couple of street friends out of jail for a few extra days? He couldn't be certain of it anymore. It was one thing for David to sleep on a sofa most nights and eat ramen noodles every day. He could manage that for a while. But it was another thing altogether for him to inadvertently put Thomas's family on the line. David had to start carrying his own weight. He owed Thomas that.

"I'm real sorry to hear about Luke Murphy," Thomas mentioned. "I know you guys were friends."

"Thanks. It's all a bit of a blur right now."

"Doc said you went to talk to this Rebel guy last night."

"Yeah."

"What did you make of him?"

"He needs some serious help."

"I hear he needs serious *psychological* help."

"Probably true. But he also needs a good lawyer."

David didn't expound. He didn't really know what else to say at the moment.

Thomas studied him. "Look, we're full partners, okay? So I will never tell you what to do or not to do. We're in this together. But just know that an unwinnable juggernaut case like this could completely break our firm right now."

On the way back to the office, David was waiting for a walk sign to cross an intersection when a shiny black Porsche 911 convertible with the top down pulled to a stop right next to him. David let his eyes take in the beauty of the vehicle. Six months ago, he could have purchased a similar ride. He certainly missed the plush leather seats and fancy dashboard of his Range Rover. He had to admit he missed the stare of strangers when sitting behind the wheel. Hell, he missed a lot of niceties about his old life.

David's eyes drifted over to the driver, and he cursed. Behind the steering wheel sat William Tidmore, his former rival at Hunter & Kellerman. The lanky lawyer with the pale skin and perfectly sculpted blond hair wore a sharp-looking gray business suit. David tried not to make direct eye contact, but it was too late. Tidmore had already spotted him on the sidewalk and seemed pleased to catch David gawking at his sports car. Tidmore peered up at him with the same cocky smile that always made David want to punch the guy right in the face.

"Hey, Trailer Park," Tidmore said, using the nickname he'd created because of David's humble upbringing. "How are things over at county court?"

David tried to keep his cool. "At least I still have my soul, Tidmore."

Tidmore laughed. "You can have your soul. I'll take the Porsche."

Tidmore then raised his right hand, casually flipped David the bird, spun the tires, and left David standing there on the sidewalk in a cloud of exhaust.

SIX

That evening, David grabbed a booth in the back of Midnight Cowboy, a narrow under-the-radar speakeasy-style bar on Sixth Street. It was happy hour, and the sidewalks outside were already buzzing as crowds of people escaped from nearby office buildings and found solace inside the city's popular hotspots. Midnight Cowboy was not David's regular place—the bar had no outside sign and was by reservation only—but his drinking partner was a bit uneasy about sitting down with him today. So he'd promised her something private, where they could talk freely without anyone from her office catching wind of it.

David had spent the afternoon pulling together more information about Rebel's case. An online criminal background check showed nothing, not even a misdemeanor, which took him a bit by surprise. He'd also privately secured the toxicology report through Lolita over at the county jail. Another surprise. No traces of drugs and only minor traces of alcohol.

David watched as a hostess led Dana Mitchem from the front. A tall black woman wearing a sleek brown business suit, Dana was an assistant district attorney who, like Murphy, had graduated from Stanford Law a year before David. Dana had had her sights set on prosecution from the beginning. Her father was a longtime judge in Louisiana, so she was comfortable in a courtroom. It was easy imagining Dana also wearing a black robe one day. She used to beat David's socks off in mock trial competitions. She was a damn good lawyer and an even better friend.

Looking weary, Dana slid into the booth across from him.

"You look like you could use a drink," David offered.

"Maybe two or three. Been a rough day. I still can't believe Murphy is gone, David. I keep expecting to wake up from this nightmare."

"Me, too. Doesn't seem real. Murphy had texted me a couple of times the past month, wanting to grab beers and catch up, but I kept pushing him off. Just been busy. Now I'll never get the chance again."

"Yeah, I keep reliving his final words to me last night as he passed by my office. *There's more to life than the law. Get out of here and go have fun.* He said that to me nearly every time he found me working late hours—which was always, of course."

"What was he doing in that alley last night, Dana? It's not like Murphy to hit the bar district after work."

"I have no clue. No one seems to know."

"Have you talked to Michelle?" David asked.

She shook her head. "Not yet. I don't even know what to say to her."

"Same here."

They ordered a couple of drinks from a waiter.

"How's everyone doing over there at the DA's office?" David asked.

"We're all reeling a bit. I think it's easy for us to disassociate ourselves from the violence and death of our day-to-day caseload until it happens right inside our own personal circle." She frowned at him. "You're not really going to represent this guy, are you, David?"

"Probably not. But I haven't made a decision yet."

"How could you? We're talking about Murphy here."

"It's complicated."

David didn't really know how to explain it all to her at this point, so he didn't even try.

"Whatever," Dana said. "Jordan's going to push for a quick indictment and trial, and he'll get it. He wants this wrapped up before the end of the year. I've already heard talk of going after the death penalty. He wants blood on this one."

Jeff Jordan was the Travis County district attorney, a pit bull of a man who played rough inside both the courts and politics. David was not a fan.

"I'm sure everyone is a bit emotional over there today."

"It's more than that," Dana countered. "He's up for reelection. Jordan hasn't exactly gotten a lot of good press this past year, if you hadn't noticed. The Malchado case was a complete disaster. There have been other foul-ups and missteps, all of which have made Jordan suddenly vulnerable. I've heard the talk around the office already. I think Jordan sees this as a chance to create some good vibes with the public that he can ride straight through an election victory."

"I hate politics."

"But this is our world, and you know that."

"Who's he putting on it?"

"Neil Mason."

"That guy's an arrogant jackass."

"But he's Jordan's number one, and he *never* loses."

"What if I wanted to plead out?"

"I thought you hadn't made a decision?"

"Hypothetically speaking," he clarified.

"Listen to me. Jordan needs this to go to trial. He wants the platform and the media spectacle. So I wouldn't expect any kind of plea offer on this case."

"What about an insanity plea?"

"Come on, David. Don't be a dumbass. You know that's like playing the lottery, because even if this guy is crazy—and from what I've read so far, that's a given—Mason will bring in every necessary medical expert to prove otherwise and get this guy to trial."

David cursed. "Did we realize how screwed up the system really was when we were back in law school?"

She smiled. "I did. I grew up in it. You guys were all naive."

"No, we just went after the money."

"How'd that work out for you?"

"Touché. But I've got stories to tell."

The waiter returned with their drinks.

Dana raised her glass. "To law school dreams."

"To Murphy."

He clinked his glass with hers. She downed hers in one gulp. He barely sipped his.

"You really should quit your job and come work with me," David said. He made the same playful offer every time they met up for drinks.

She rolled her eyes. "Whatever. You're so broke, you have to sleep on your office sofa every night."

"It's true. And becoming more broke by the day, it seems. Thomas just informed me that I only bring in thirteen percent of the firm's monthly income. How pathetic is that?"

"Quite pathetic," she teased.

"I'm working more than I did over at H&K. Just with clients that can't pay. That's why I need you. If I put your face up on our crappy website, we'd have paying clients lined up out the door. All my problems would be over."

They shared a quick laugh. Something they needed right now.

"Is that why we're talking about this case?" Dana asked, turning serious again. "Is this about lawyer fees? Does this guy have money hidden somewhere?"

David shook his head. "Not that I know about."

She arched an eyebrow. "Wait . . . Please tell me you don't actually think he's innocent?"

"Of course not. Just playing devil's advocate."

He didn't feel like explaining Rebel's connection with Benny and the strange pull David felt inside to somehow help the guy—even if he was guilty. He'd come across so many new friends during the past year who operated in a different mental reality because living out on the streets over time had brutally assaulted their once-stable minds.

"Good," Dana replied. "Because we already have everything we need. We've got his prints on the gun. We have a witness who saw him toss the weapon and run. We have him admitting he fired the weapon in the alley. We even have sidewalk security video showing him following Murphy into the alley only moments before he was shot."

"Really?" It was the first David had heard of a security video. "Have you seen this sidewalk video?"

"Yes. Why?"

"Does it show his face? Can you definitely say it's him?"

"Well, no, not exactly. It was taken from behind. But he's wearing the same green jacket and black hat that witnesses saw him wearing when he fled the scene."

"I see. So someone else could have worn it into the alley?"

"You're buying the whole blackout thing?"

"Just humor me, okay?"

"Fine, but this is getting annoying. Yes, someone else could have worn the outfit into the alley."

"And the guy has no criminal record," David added.

"True," Dana said. "But a jury won't care. There's a first time for everything."

"Have you established any connection between Murphy and the accused?"

"Not that I'm aware of. Not sure we even need to do that."

"What about the toxicology report?"

"No traces of drugs," she admitted.

"And only *minor* traces of alcohol," he followed up. "What about Murphy's possessions? Did you find anything belonging to Murphy on him? Wallet? Watch? *Anything?*"

"No," she replied.

"So why did he shoot him, Dana? For fun?"

She shrugged. "Who the hell knows? Maybe the CIA told him to do it. Or perhaps it was the Russians. Better yet, it was the aliens. They told him to do it. We've got a lot to choose from, believe me. Besides, I've seen a lot of people do really violent things for no good reason at all over the past two years."

SEVEN

David was led to the same private jail room where he'd met with Rebel the previous night. Sitting in the chair opposite him, Rebel seemed much more subdued—even defeated. The wild look that had been so prominent in his eyes last night had all but disappeared. Instead, he seemed foggy and disengaged, and David wondered if a jail doctor had sedated him. He wouldn't be surprised, considering Rebel's frantic state of mind at the tail end of their last meeting. There was a swollen bump above his right eye and a few scrapes on his right cheek that weren't there the last time they were together. Was that the work of jailhouse deputies or inmates? Could a guy like Rebel even survive a lengthy jail stay?

David asked the deputy to remove the handcuffs. The deputy seemed reluctant, but David assured him he'd be fine. He hoped the move would show Rebel a bit of trust, and in return, Rebel might open up to David. When the deputy left them alone in the room, David finally sat across the table from the man.

"How're you doing, Rebel?"

Rebel shrugged, kept his eyes on the table. "Been better, Lawyer."

"They treating you okay in here?"

"Don't matter. They taking me back to the dragon's lair soon."

His speech was slow and lacked any real punch, which was opposite of how he'd been talking last night.

"Where is this dragon's lair?" David asked.

"Can't talk about it. That would only make it worse for me."

"Who said you were going back?"

"No one had to tell me, Lawyer. I just know. This ain't my first rodeo. I've been a cowboy a long time. I can tell by the way everyone looks at me. This deal has already been done. Might as well give 'em what they all want and get this whole thing over with more quickly."

"What do they want?"

"My confession."

"Why would you confess to something you say you didn't do?"

Rebel put his hands on the table, touched his fingers together. "Maybe I did do it."

David tilted his head. "Did you?"

Rebel gave a nonchalant shrug, didn't elaborate. "Don't even matter anymore."

"I can't help you if you won't talk to me."

"You can't help me anyway, Lawyer. I done told you that already. You can't stop it. No one can stop it. I already seen a couple of spooks wearing trench coats in here, watching me through the bars, talking to the uniforms, working it all out. They taking me back to the dragon's lair soon."

Easing back in his chair, David tried to see if he could get Rebel talking about something else, an effort to distract him, maybe pull the truth out another way. Although David couldn't be sure if the man even knew the truth.

"Why do they call you Rebel?"

For the first time, the man's eyes lifted. A small grin appeared, a hint of a spark. "You ever seen that old James Dean movie?"

"*Rebel Without a Cause?*"

He nodded, the grin firming up now. "You see, I was trying to date this girl back in high school. Well, she was in high school. I was a bit older. Norma Jean. Man, was she ever a looker. But her granny didn't like me too much. Wanted me to stay the hell away from her. Always chasing me off with a broomstick. Don't blame her. I was a real trouble-maker. She said I reminded her of James Dean in that old movie, so she started calling me *Rebel*."

"Did you stay away from the girl?"

The grin eased into a sly smile. "Whatcha think, Lawyer?"

David laughed. "I had a feeling."

"My idiot buddies all thought the nickname was funny, so it kind of stuck around. Funny how nicknames can come about."

"Benny called me *Shep*. Said I reminded him of a shepherd in the Bible. So now everyone on the streets calls me that."

"*Rebel* is a helluva lot better than *Shep*, I tell you what."

"Can't argue with that."

They shared a quick laugh. Rebel's was more of a loud cackle—a sudden burst where his shoulders bounced up and down. He looked so free when he let it out. For a moment, David could see what Benny must've seen in this man. If you could somehow get past the conspiracy chaos, there was something endearing about him.

Rebel seemed to still be thinking more about his youth. "Those were the good old days, Lawyer, I tell you what. Fast cars, lots of smok-ing, drinking, and having a good time. I rode up the California coast once with James Dean. He had himself a fast little sports car. The girls actually liked me more than him, but that was before he became a big movie star."

David pinched his mouth. James Dean had died more than thirty years before Rebel was even born. What kind of wires were crossed up in his brain that placed thoughts like that inside? He didn't bring it up since the conversation had lifted Rebel's spirits.

"I went to law school in Northern California," David mentioned.

"I love that place. Beautiful beaches and gorgeous women. I would have stayed in Cali a long time if I hadn't joined the program."

"What program?"

He looked over at David, as if catching himself. "Can't talk about it, Lawyer."

"Seems there's a lot of things you can't talk about."

"Not unless you want to go where I'm going. Trust me, you don't."

"Okay. What about family? Got any brothers and sisters?"

"Nope. Mom had trouble at my birth. Couldn't have more kids after me."

"You got any kids? You mentioned being married once."

"A son," Rebel revealed, before a bit of sadness returned to his eyes. "I ain't seen the boy in a long time." He stared at his hands, seemed to be counting his fingers. "Hell, he's probably six by now."

"What's your son's name?"

This brought on a small smile. "Roger Junior. A beautiful little boy with a fighting spirit about him. Like his daddy." The smile slowly faded. "Just wish my mother had been around to see my boy. She died when I was a kid."

"My mother also died when I was young. What about your father?"

Rebel shrugged. "Never knew the man. He was long gone by the time I could walk and talk. After my mother died, I was mostly raised on my uncle's ranch in Arkansas. My uncle never had any kids. He was a hard man but did the best he could with me. He died when I was serving over in Iraq. My uncle told me my father got stabbed to death in prison a few years after he'd left my mom."

"I barely remember my father, too. He died in a car wreck when I was six."

They shared a long stare, an exchange of both sorrow and understanding.

"Well, look at us, Lawyer. Two peas in a pod, you and me."

"I guess so."

"Only I'm sitting here locked up in chains, while you're out there walking around a free man. I guess that's the way the wind blows sometimes."

David thought about that for a moment. He knew his life could've turned out more like the man sitting in front of him had his sister, Brandy, not been there for him as a safety net. After their mother's unexpected death when he was a teenager, David had quickly spiraled down a path of self-destruction. Drugs, theft, fistfights. He would have likely ended up in a jail cell somewhere had his big sister not dropped out of college, moved back home, and dragged him kicking and screaming out of the gutter. He owed everything he was today to Brandy. David thought about what Jen, who had done advocacy work with the homeless, had told him last year: *The single greatest cause of homelessness is a profound, catastrophic loss of family.* That appeared to be a big part of Rebel's tragic story. When the wheels came off, he did not have a big-sister safety net to catch his fall.

"You really buy that property I heard about?" Rebel asked him.

David raised an eyebrow, surprised. But then, he knew word got around out on the streets. "Yeah, I did. Twenty acres."

"Whatcha doin' with it?"

"Nothing at the moment."

"Why?"

"I'm broke. It takes money to develop a big property like that."

"Benny really wanted to build a village out there?"

"Yeah, he did. My plan is to follow through on it—someday."

Rebel nodded. "Can I ask you a favor? In case I never get out of here."

"Okay, what?"

"Find my dog and take care of him." Rebel's eyes began watering up, surprising David. "He's probably out there cold, scared, and starving without me around. I need someone to look after him. He's all I've got, Lawyer."

"Where do I find him?"

"Over near Pease Park . . . Wait, he's probably under the First Street Bridge . . . No, that ain't right, either." Rebel seemed to be racking his brain and getting frustrated, as if he couldn't remember where exactly he'd been staying before all this happened to him. "He's over by the South Shore Apartments . . . Wait . . . dammit!"

"Take it easy, Rebel. What's your dog look like?"

"Just a mutt, kind of like me. Not much to him. Brown with a big white spot on his back that kind of looks like a star. He's a sweet little thing, but he'll tear your damn leg off you try to mess with me while I'm sleeping."

"What's your dog's name?"

"Sandy—my father's name."

"I'll do my best to find him."

Checking his watch, David leaned forward on his elbows. It was getting late, so it was time to get serious again. He couldn't sit there all night talking about the good old days or Rebel's dog. It did no one any good to keep dragging this out.

"You have a hearing before a judge tomorrow, Rebel. That's when the official charges will be brought against you. They'll ask you how you want to plead to the charges—guilty, not guilty, or no contest."

"What happens if I say I'm guilty?"

"They'll probably give you life in prison without parole."

"The dragon's lair, you mean."

"I guess."

"And what happens if I say I'm not guilty?"

"You'll go to trial."

"And if I lose the trial?"

David swallowed, didn't really want to answer that question. But Rebel seemed to read through his silence.

"I see. They stick me with the needle." He sat all the way back in his chair, contemplating that. "Don't seem like very good options to me."

"It's going to be a tough road either way."

"Will you be there tomorrow?" Rebel asked.

"Do you want me to be there?"

Rebel shrugged. "You can't be all bad if Benny liked you."

David knew that was Rebel's roundabout way of asking him to be his lawyer without having to directly say it. "What will you say to the judge tomorrow, Rebel?"

"You my lawyer?"

"Not yet."

"Then I guess you'll have to show up to find out."

EIGHT

David slipped out a back exit of the jailhouse, just like he had the previous night. Although he hadn't spotted any TV reporters standing outside the front door upon his arrival earlier, he still didn't want to take any chances. Murphy's death had been the lead story all day on the local news. He really didn't want to deal with the media yet—or ever, for that matter. He still didn't know what he was going to do about representing Rebel. The man seemed resigned to take whatever punishment was coming for him, even if that amounted to a confession. At this point, David wasn't sure Rebel even knew whether he was guilty. There was so much misinformation stored inside his foggy head.

How could David defend someone like that? Especially if what Dana had told him earlier was true: that the DA would not be offering a plea deal and would fight tooth and nail against any type of insanity plea. As much as David empathized with the guy—especially now knowing they'd shared similar life tragedies—Dana was right. The whole thing felt like a no-win situation. Not to mention the negative financial impact it could have on the firm if David found himself completely tied up in this case the next few months instead of pursuing paying clients. He just couldn't do that to Thomas. He knew he had to walk away from this thing.

David was ten paces down the sidewalk from the criminal justice complex when someone stepped out of the shadows right in front of him. He paused, a bit startled, stared at a woman in her twenties wearing blue jeans, tennis shoes, and a gray hoodie pulled way up over her head. She reminded him a bit of Jen—both had pretty green eyes. But this girl's eyes were bouncing everywhere—behind David, over her own shoulder, left, right, and back again, as if she were paranoid as hell. Hands shoved deep inside the hoodie's front pockets, she kept shifting her weight back and forth. David wondered if she was high on drugs or something.

"Are you the homeless guy's lawyer?" she quietly asked him.

"You okay?" David asked.

"Are you his lawyer?" she repeated, ignoring his concern.

David played dumb. "What homeless guy?"

"The one they say murdered the prosecutor in the alley last night."

David's eyes narrowed. "Who are you?"

"No one." She looked over her shoulder again.

"Then why're you asking me about it?"

"I just . . . I don't . . . I just need to know, okay?"

David wasn't sure how she could've possibly known he was talking to Rebel, but he had no desire to stand there and chat with a stranger about a case that wasn't even his at this point.

"Look, it's late," David said, brushing her off. "Have a good night, okay?"

He stepped around her, began walking away.

"There's more to the story," she said from behind him.

He stopped in his tracks, spun back around.

"More to what story?" he asked.

She shifted awkwardly. "With the homeless guy who was arrested."

Now it was David's turn to look around, wondering what the hell was going on. "What do you know about it?"

"Are you his lawyer?"

"Maybe. Who are you?"

"I told you, I'm no one."

"Then what's this all about?"

She crossed her arms, constantly fidgeting. "I can't say . . . I don't . . . I don't know what to do."

"If you know something, I need you to tell me right now. A man's life could be on the line here."

"So could mine!" she snapped back.

David saw a flash of anger in her eyes that took him off guard. "What do you mean?"

She exhaled, swallowed. "I saw him last night, okay?"

"Who?"

Their conversation was abruptly interrupted when a group of four uniformed officers walked up the sidewalk toward them from a county garage that sat directly across the street from the criminal justice complex. The sight of them approaching made the woman immediately shut down their exchange. She quickly sidestepped David and took off at a brisk pace up the sidewalk.

"Wait a second!" David called after her, took a few steps forward in pursuit. "Please talk to me. Who did you see?"

She didn't stop. Instead, she began to run at a full sprint and disappeared around an adjacent building. David thought about chasing after her but decided against it. That might look odd to the police. Besides, she could just be another crazy person. The city was full of them. Still—something told him she wasn't.

And that left his gut seriously churning.

Twenty minutes later, David gently knocked on the front door of a quaint one-story redbrick house on a nice neighborhood street in South Austin. Thomas answered right away in sweatpants and a T-shirt, stepped outside to join David on the sidewalk.

"Hope I didn't wake the kids," David offered.

"No chance. My girls sleep like logs once they're finally out. Of course, it usually takes us an hour to get them to be still and go to sleep. What's so urgent?"

"I need to talk to you about Rebel's case."

"Yeah, I figured. What about it?"

"Well, I was ready to drop it. Like we talked about. In spite of my desire to try to somehow help the guy. But then something just happened outside the county jail that has me reconsidering things."

David went on to explain his bizarre interaction with the woman.

"She just ran away?" Thomas asked. "Why?"

"I wish I knew. But she was clearly spooked."

"Who do you think she was talking about?"

David shrugged. "Rebel? Murphy? I can't be sure."

"Why are you taking her so seriously? She could be a whack job."

"A gut feeling."

Thomas sighed, shook his head. "Didn't they teach you not to rely on gut feelings in law school? Your gut will get you into a lot of trouble, believe me."

"I must've missed that day."

"You really think the guy could somehow be innocent?"

"Before what just happened, I was ninety-nine percent sure he was guilty. Now, well, I'm a little less sure."

"What if Rebel walks into that courtroom tomorrow and pleads guilty?"

"No harm, no foul. I'll do my best to work out good prison terms for him, and we quickly move on with the business of the firm. But what if he pleads not guilty?"

"We'll have a huge mess on our hands."

"Look, Thomas, I would never do this without your blessing. I know how disruptive it could be right now for our firm. But *something* is pulling me into this. I can't explain it."

Thomas crossed his arms, stared out toward the street a long moment. Finally, he said, "Hell, we didn't start this firm to play it safe. We'll figure it out."

David grinned. "You mean it?"

"Yes. Let's just hope your stupid gut is right."

NINE

Rebel's court hearing was scheduled for eight the next morning in a small courtroom inside the criminal justice complex. Wearing a blue suit and tie and holding his briefcase, David waited until the very last minute to slip inside the building, which was buzzing with more energy than he'd seen over the past six months. A stable of TV reporters was lined up out front, hair and makeup perfect, microphones in hands, cameras rolling, a half dozen news channel trucks parked up and down the street. Inside, the courtroom was jam-packed with people, with several more photographers shooting video around the perimeter of the room. Although this was only a standard court hearing, like many throughout the day, it already had the feel of the trial of the year. Which caused more butterflies to flutter inside David's stomach.

Squeezing into the back of the noisy courtroom, David looked around, wondered about all the other people who'd somehow found their way inside. He'd never seen most of them in the building. Up front, he spotted Neil Mason, the DA's right-hand man, his thick head of sculpted black hair perfectly matching his sleek black suit. In his late forties, Mason had been with the DA's office for more than ten years, where he'd tried and won several high-profile murder cases. At six-three, he had the build of a former linebacker and a South Texas drawl that seemed to play well with jurors. Most figured he was next in line for DA—*if* Jordan won the election next year and served out another term. David hadn't had too much interaction with Mason—most of David's clients were being prosecuted for low-level misdemeanors—but their few brief interactions had never left a good taste in his mouth. Mason seemed very comfortable with his reputation for being a pompous ass.

Taking a deep breath and exhaling slowly, David pushed his way through the small crowd at the back and made his way up to the front, where he set down his briefcase beside the defense table. He felt all eyes in the room lock in on him, including the fierce gaze of Mason. They exchanged a quick nod of recognition, like two boxers tapping gloves before round one.

The courtroom suddenly quieted as Judge Alison Marvis took her seat behind the bench. With curly gray hair and thick glasses, Judge Marvis was an experienced jurist who was known to be fair and considerate. She welcomed everyone, and the room quickly came to order. At that point, Mason brought the case before Judge Marvis, and Rebel, wearing the standard jail jumpsuit with his hands and feet both cuffed, was led into the courtroom from a side door by a buff bailiff who looked ready to put him in a choke hold at any moment. The bailiff shuffled him over in front of the judge's bench before settling him right next to David. The homeless man looked over, seemed surprised. David had not taken the opportunity to meet with Rebel beforehand. There was really nothing more to say. He knew Rebel could tell him one thing in advance and then do the opposite in front of the judge. David figured he'd just let the hearing play out and go from there.

"You find my dog?" Rebel whispered.

David almost laughed. Not because he thought it was funny. The man was about to be charged with murder, and the first thing out of his mouth upon seeing his new lawyer was a question about his dog. It was a last-second reminder about the insanity David might be walking into by representing this guy.

"Not yet."

"Why not? I'm worried sick."

"I'll look around today, okay? Now pay attention to the judge."

Judge Marvis then read the official charges against Rebel. First-degree murder in the death of Lucas Murphy.

"How do you plead, Mr. North?" the judge asked Rebel.

It was the first time David had ever stood next to a client in a courtroom where he didn't know what they'd actually say to the judge.

Rebel stood straighter, chest out. "Not guilty, Your Honor."

David exhaled. He didn't even realize he'd been holding his breath. A sudden burst of adrenaline began coursing through him. Judge Marvis acknowledged Rebel's plea for the court. David heard murmurs from the crowd. Everything just got serious.

David jumped back into the conversation. "Your Honor, we'd like to request bail. My client is not a flight risk."

Mason quickly countered. "On the contrary, Your Honor, Mr. North is known as a drifter with a history of leaving town on a whim. Our doctors also believe he is dangerously unstable."

"Denied, Mr. Adams," the judge ruled, as expected.

"Thank you, Your Honor," David replied.

David knew that bail was never going to be an option. Not that Rebel had any money to post it, anyway. But it was a formality for him to ask and advocate for his client. Judge Marvis ordered Rebel to remain locked up in the county facility while he awaited his next court date, which she set for two weeks away. She then touched down her gavel. The hearing was over, and even louder chatter began all around the courtroom again.

Rebel turned to him. "Why'd you come, Lawyer?"

"Maybe I'm as crazy as you."

This brought on a small grin. "Two peas in a pod, you and me."

"I'll be in to see you soon, okay?"

"Well, I sure as hell ain't going nowhere."

The bailiff then led his client out of the courtroom by the same side door.

Grabbing his briefcase, David turned, faced Mason for the first time. Mason gave him a smug grin.

"Welcome to the big leagues, Mr. Adams. You sure you're ready?"

"Nope. But I'll be by your office this afternoon to discuss the case."

"Make an appointment. I'm a very busy man."

David then watched as Mason left the courtroom and walked straight into a wave of reporters in the hallway. David didn't follow. Instead, he slipped out a side door and hoped to somehow navigate his way out of the building without talking to anyone. Smart or not, he was now all in on this case, so it was time to roll up his sleeves and get to work.

TEN

David hightailed it back to his office with a renewed purpose in his step. He had to immediately begin his own investigation to see if there was any truth to the mystery woman's claim—that there was more to the story behind Rebel's arrest. As far-fetched as it still seemed, David had to work with the hypothetical that Rebel did not in fact shoot and kill his friend. Which meant someone else did. Who? Why? According to Dana, the DA's office wasn't all that interested in finding another suspect. They were convinced they already had their guy and were eager to go to trial. David's only hope was to go out there himself and find the real killer—or *at least* find enough evidence to place huge question marks around the certainty his client pulled the trigger. That prospect felt daunting at the moment. He was just one man, and this was a big city. Unlike other more high-profile defense firms, Gray & Adams, LLP couldn't afford to hire real investigators. That hadn't mattered too much over the past six months, since most of his cases were simple misdemeanors. But it sure as hell mattered now. His client's life was on the line.

Reaching his building, he bounded up the stairs two at a time and turned the corner toward his office suite. As usual, Bobby E. Lee was sitting in a chair right outside the front door, wearing his gray

Confederate-soldier outfit. The white-bearded black man stood and saluted upon David's arrival, just like he did nearly every time David came in and out of the office.

"Morning, Bobby," David said.

Bobby Lee acknowledged him with a simple nod of the head. David opened the office door, stepped inside, and was surprised to find several of the boys from the Camp waiting for him in the entry room. Doc stood against the wall, arms crossed, looking pleased. His paralegal had gotten what he'd wanted—David's help with Rebel. Larue sat in one of the chairs at the table. A young black man of about twenty with his hair in cornrows, he wore baggy jeans with a red Chicago Bulls jersey. Curly, a man in his forties with a wild mop of brown hair, sat in another chair, wearing his usual denim jacket, jeans, and work boots. Shifty occupied the final chair. The seventysomething man had white wisps of hair and was missing half his teeth. But he was still doing his best to devour the contents of a leftover box of glazed doughnuts. This group of men had remained David's closest crew since the Camp had met its unfortunate demise last year.

Thomas stepped out from his office to quietly greet David.

"Watched the news," Thomas said. "Guess we're getting the huge mess."

"Hope I'm right."

"Me, too."

"What's everyone doing here?" David asked.

"I asked Doc to round them all up. Figured we could use all the help we could get."

David looked around the room. Had any client ever been represented by a more misfit legal team? He shook his head. Rebel might be doomed. "Hey, guys. Appreciate you coming to the office this morning. I'm sure Doc has already gotten you up to speed, but here's the deal. As of this morning, Rebel has been officially charged with first-degree murder. I need your help to prove that he's innocent."

"We're here for you, Shep," Shifty chimed in, glazed icing all over his lips.

"Yeah, man," Curly concurred in his husky voice. "Whatever you need."

"Just tell us what to do, bro," added Larue.

David began to pace the room in a tight circle. "Rebel can't remember much about the other night. He claims he's suffered from blackout spells for years, where he can be completely out of it for up to thirty minutes, and he says that's exactly what happened to him. He woke up in the alley wearing someone else's jacket and hat, and then found a gun in his pocket. Next thing he knows, he's being arrested. I need your help to retrace his steps in the hours leading up to his arrest. I need to know where he was, what he was doing, who he was talking to, anything and everything we can find that might shine some light on what really happened."

"I know some guys that used to hang with Rebel," Curly said. "I'll see if I can track any of them down. Maybe they know something."

Larue jumped in. "Yeah, I know a lot of dudes that hang out right by that same alley, since I'm always over at Pete's. I'll see what I can find out."

Larue was a bit of a music savant. Benny had taken him under his wing. The old man had helped the kid break the bondage of addiction and had given him a chance to grow his musical talent. Because of that, Larue had earned himself a part-time gig over at Pete's Dueling Piano Bar on Sixth, a sing-along joint with a stage that hosted two of the city's best ivory ticklers in a nightly battle. David had gone there to watch Larue on several occasions. He could play like no one David had ever heard.

"Appreciate that, Larue and Curly," David said. "Anyone have any idea where Rebel has been staying? He can't seem to remember that, either."

"He used to camp by himself over by the greenbelt across from the mall," Shifty said. "But I ain't seen him around there in a long time."

"I don't think he stays *anywhere* for too long," Doc said. "A night or two here and there before he moves along. He's always been a bit paranoid *someone* was going to find him. I believe the month he was with us at the Camp was the longest he'd ever been stationary."

David considered that. "Well, we need to find the last place he was staying. Not only could it offer a look into what Rebel was doing, but I need to find his dog. I think the dog has Rebel even more concerned than going on trial."

"I remember that little yapper," Shifty said, smiling, revealing a gaping hole where two front teeth were missing. "That mutt kept waking me up in the middle of the night. Yap, yap, yap!"

"You remember what the dog looks like, Shifty?" David asked.

"Yeah, think so. Name is Sandy, right?"

"Correct. You run point on finding the dog."

"Yes, boss."

The boys all seemed eager to help, which David appreciated. The more eyes and ears he had around town, the better. After they'd all left, David moved inside his office. The TV was on and showing the local news channel. He immediately spotted video of himself standing right next to Rebel inside the courtroom. When the reporter directly mentioned him by name, David grabbed the remote and turned off the TV.

"Just going to get crazier," Thomas said from the doorway. "I've already fielded a dozen media calls here at the office. Some of them have already put together that you and Murphy went to law school together. Everyone wants to know why you're doing it."

"Tell them the ghost of Benny told me to do it."

"Right. That'll make them leave us alone."

"What do you know about Neil Mason?"

"Tough SOB. Doesn't play nice."

"I'm going by to see him this afternoon and talk about the case."

"Want me to come along?"

David shook his head. "Nah, I'm good. I can handle him."

"I've already filed paperwork to get you access to the crime scene and other matters."

"Thanks. I've got to find out what Murphy was doing in that alley the other night. Doesn't make any sense—and no one seems to know for sure."

"What else can I do?"

"First things first: take good care of your paying clients. Try to keep our doors open while I roll the dice with our firm's future."

Thomas sighed. "Yeah, about those doors."

He handed David a folded sheet of white paper. Opening it, David immediately spotted the words *Eviction Notice* printed at the top.

"You've got to be kidding me?" David said.

Had his sleeping on the sofa brought on the eviction notice?

Thomas took a seat in a guest chair. "Found it stuck to the door when I came in this morning. Apparently, our building is under new ownership. And I guess the new owners don't like us as tenants very much."

David skimmed the notice again. "It says we've violated a clause in our lease agreement but doesn't specify anything."

Thomas shrugged. "I don't know. I called and set up a meeting to discuss it with them in person tomorrow."

"I'll be there, too."

"You have more important matters right now."

"Listen, Thomas, if we're looking at getting kicked out of this office because I'm the idiot who's been sleeping on the sofa every night and violating our terms, then I'll sure as hell be there to beg them for forgiveness."

ELEVEN

David knew it was critical to get a good look at the crime scene as soon as possible. Considering the DA's current position with the case, the police would not likely keep the alley under lockdown for too much longer. Not when they already had their guy in custody and a half dozen popular bars along the building strip needed access to the alley to operate every night. David showed legal papers to a portly police officer who guarded the barricaded perimeter on one end of the alley and seemed bored out of his mind. Staring a half block down the street, David noted that Murphy's white Escape was still parked along the curb, looking unnoticed and untouched.

The officer shoved the paperwork back at him. "All righty, pal. Don't touch or remove anything."

"Anything else I should know?"

The officer shrugged. "The orange cones mark where they found the body."

Slipping around the barricades, David moved into the alley, which reeked of a pungent cocktail of beer, vomit, and urine. He took note of the various dirty dumpsters and all sorts of homeless remnants that led him to believe the alley was a popular overnight sleeping spot. Worn blankets, old clothes, and box debris were littered throughout and cluttered up back doorways to the building strip. Did any of the items belong to Rebel? Was anyone else sleeping in the alley near Rebel the night of the murder? He knew Mason wouldn't have his own investigators spend much time trying to track down a homeless eyewitness. Not only would most of David's street friends never talk to the police, they weren't usually credible enough to use in a courtroom, anyway. David hoped his own investigative crew could find a diamond in the rough.

Stepping up to the orange cones that framed the placement of Murphy's body, David felt a sudden catch in his throat. It was hard to imagine that his friend's life had been taken right there in that spot by a sudden bullet to the back of the head. What was Murphy doing in the alley? Was he cutting through on his way from or back to his vehicle? Did he simply find himself in the wrong place at the wrong time? Or was there more to it?

Kneeling, David could see the stain of blood on the pavement. His eyes grew moist when thinking about Michelle and the kids. Several times over the past two days, he'd thought about picking up the phone and offering her his condolences, but he couldn't get himself to make the call just yet. Especially now that he was officially representing Rebel. What would she be thinking now that David had agreed to defend the man who all Murphy's colleagues thought was guilty?

David stood and glanced over toward the back door of Burnside's Tavern, only a few feet away. He'd spoken on the phone a couple of minutes ago with the same bar employee from the police report, who basically reiterated verbatim everything he'd said to the police that night. He stepped out for a smoke, spotted the dead body, and then heard a gun being fired maybe twenty feet away. He called 911 while watching a man wearing a green military-style jacket and a black knit hat toss something into a dumpster before running out of the alley. That was it. There was nothing flaky about his account of things. Although he did confirm that he saw others running out of the alley around the same time as the man in the green jacket.

David again wondered about the woman who had approached him outside the jail last night. *There's more to the story.* Did she really know anything? Or was she just another wacko? Since news had broken of his representation, David had already received several voice mails from strangers who all claimed to know something about the case—none of which had panned out as legitimate. One man claimed he had proof that Rebel was working directly for Don Vito Corleone. A city of crazies.

Walking over to the back door of the tavern, David stood directly where the witness must've stood the other night. He peered down at the orange cones, then all the way up the alley. There was nothing blocking his view. No dumpsters, no debris. The witness had a direct line of sight. David stepped all the way to the opposite end of the alley from where he'd entered, looking around to see if he noticed anything that might be helpful. Nothing stood out. Sixth Street was busy every single night of the week. Surely *someone* had to have seen *something.* The problem for him was that the police already had their man. So if anyone had spotted Murphy here or there, or had seen something peculiar, there was no official call to action to report it. David had to go find them.

Looking up at the surrounding buildings, David wondered from which end of the alley the police had snagged the sidewalk security video that apparently showed Murphy entering the alley and being followed by someone wearing a green jacket. He'd find that out when he got discovery material from Mason that afternoon. Moving back through the alley again, he took several photos on his cell phone, documenting everything. He would show them all to Rebel, see if he could trigger anything from the man's shoddy memory vault.

Finished, David sidestepped the barricades again and thanked the police officer, who only grunted at him and went back to staring at his cell phone. David casually walked the half block over to Murphy's Escape. There was a parking ticket under the windshield wiper. Glancing inside the back seat window, he noticed that Murphy had a black gym bag, along with two booster seats for his kids. David took a peek inside the front window, saw two empty coffee cups in the console. Folded up in the front passenger seat was a gray suit jacket, which Murphy must've been wearing on that day.

David squinted, noticing something else in the passenger seat. Poking out from under the jacket was a small black leather day planner. Murphy had always been a bit old school. Could he have kept his schedule in the day planner instead of on his cell phone? Would there be anything inside that could be useful?

Circling the vehicle to the passenger side, David put his hand on the door handle, pulled, but it was locked. Back in college, Murphy had kept a key magnet under the back bumper. He'd always reach for it after they'd played pickup basketball. Could it still be there? Moving to the back of the car, he knelt, casually reached under, and felt around. His fingers landed on a small metal square. Bingo. He pulled off the magnet, found a car key fob inside.

Walking back over to the passenger door, he hit the button on the fob, heard the door locks release. He took a glance up the street at the police officer, whose eyes were still planted on his phone. Murphy's car clearly wasn't part of the investigation at this point. But David wanted to be careful being spotted doing something like this in case the vehicle ever became part of the case. Opening the door, he quickly snagged the black day planner, locked the door again, and hustled down the sidewalk.

TWELVE

David grabbed a table in the back corner of Houndstooth Coffee, which sat directly across the street from his office building. Then he began to pore through every detail of Murphy's day planner. He found a photo of Murphy with his family at Walt Disney World stuck inside the opening flap. Cinderella's castle sat in the background. Murphy looked happy, even with Mickey Mouse ears stuck on his head. The kids, of course, looked ecstatic. David knew the family had taken the trip to Orlando last summer. Murphy had told David he'd emptied out his savings account for it, since he'd been feeling guilty about how much time he was at the office these days.

Continuing to search, David found a small stack of business cards, most of which belonged to other attorneys around the city. There was even a business card for David Adams, Gray & Adams, LLP. When he'd first handed it to Murphy last fall, his friend had given him a sly grin and said he couldn't wait for their first courtroom showdown. That would never happen now.

Damn, Murphy. What were you doing in that alley?

He began flipping through the opening pages of the planner. He quickly perused a notes section, all handwritten notes Murphy must've kept on his cases over the past year. David tried to find anything that could've somehow been connected to his death. Working in the DA's office could be dangerous. There was always the possibility of a disgruntled family member taking vengeance into their own hands because a prosecutor had put a relative behind bars. David wondered if that could be the case with Murphy. Nothing stood out as obvious, but he'd give the notes to Doc to do some cross-checking. Doc was a whiz at that kind of thing.

David found a calendar in the back. It looked like Murphy kept most of his appointments listed in the day planner. Flipping to two days ago, the day of his friend's death, David scanned the entire day with his finger. Murphy had meetings and court appointments throughout the day, none of which seemed outside of normal prosecutor work. His finger then settled on ten o'clock that night, and his eyes narrowed. Thirty minutes before his death, Murphy had a meeting scribbled down with someone listed only by the initials *KP* at a bar a block over from where he'd died called the Dirty Dog. Who was KP?

He was pulled away from his thoughts by someone suddenly standing over him.

"David Adams?"

David looked up, noticed a fiftysomething man with a graying crew cut, square brown glasses, and a black windbreaker and jeans.

"Yes?" David replied.

"Keith Carter," the man said. "Sorry to interrupt. You're the attorney representing Roger North?"

David nodded. "What can I do for you?"

"I work with Texas Veterans Legal Assistance Project. We offer legal help to veterans in low-income situations. Roger North came onto our radar today."

Carter handed David a simple white business card. It listed his name, the organization's name, and an address in Austin, with an American flag logo in the background.

"I guess word travels fast," David said. "What kind of help?"

"Legal counsel. Administrative support. Legwork on the ground. That sort of thing."

"Money?"

"I wish. To be honest, donations barely cover our cheap office space."

David was disappointed to hear that. He could use whatever financial support he could get right now. "Do you have a team?"

Carter grinned. "One-man team."

"Just you?"

"Yep."

"Are you a lawyer?"

"No, sir. I just care about our vets, that's all. I know firsthand how the trauma of being in combat can mess up our military brothers' minds, which can often lead to serious legal situations. Does he really think he's being framed by the CIA or by Russian agents?"

"Who told you that?"

Carter shrugged. "I've made insider friends doing my kind of work."

"I see. I'm sure you understand I'm not at liberty to discuss my client conversations with you at this point."

"Yeah, I hear ya. Well, you have my card, Mr. Adams."

"I do, thanks."

Watching him walk away, David wondered if a guy like Carter could add any value to his investigating team. He'd keep his card handy just in case.

THIRTEEN

Even though David was on time for his four o'clock appointment with Neil Mason, he was forced to sit for thirty minutes in an uncomfortable chair down the hallway from the man's spacious corner office—like a troubled schoolkid waiting to meet with the principal. David was certain Mason was just messing with him. Several times the prosecutor had walked out into the hallway, glanced over at him, made casual conversation with others, and then strolled back inside his office.

Frustrated, David tried to make the most of his wait time. He again pored through every word written down inside Murphy's day planner, looking to somehow match up the initials KP. There was no one listed on any of the contact pages with those same initials. Who the hell was Murphy meeting with at the Dirty Dog the night of his death? David planned to make it over to the bar when it opened tonight.

Finally, a female assistant of some sort came to get David, guided him down the hallway and inside Mason's office. Mason had his suit jacket off, tie loosened, and shiny dress shoes up on the corner of his desk. David was not surprised when the man didn't bother getting up to offer any sort of greeting. But he *was* surprised to find his friend Dana standing over by the window, arms crossed, almost looking guilty for being there.

"Sorry for all the waiting," Mason offered weakly. "I believe you know Ms. Mitchem. She will be assisting me with this case."

David looked over at Dana, who gave him a slight eye roll. Clearly, she was being used as an extra pawn to somehow throw David off his game. Dana did not look at all happy about it. Maybe he could work that in his favor somehow.

"Have a seat," Mason said, motioning to a guest chair.

Sitting, David placed his briefcase on the floor. He noticed several framed photographs on the shelf behind the prosecutor's desk of Mason posing with prominent political figures. One with Mason shaking hands with the governor. Another of Mason with the mayor, both wearing baseball uniforms, arms over each other's shoulders, as if they'd just finished playing a game. David again remembered what Dana had told him yesterday—this case was as much about next year's election as it was about seeking justice. He felt his stomach turn.

"You want coffee or something?" Mason offered, picking up a miniature football off his desk. He tossed it in the air before catching it.

"No, I just want to talk about the case."

"Well, slow down a moment. Let's get to know each other better first. Dana said you played a little college ball over in Abilene."

"Yes," David replied in a deadpan manner. "My favorite color is blue. My favorite food is cheeseburgers. Can we just get to the case?"

Mason ignored that response. "I played some college ball myself over at Sam Houston. Second team all-conference tight end my senior year."

"Congratulations," David managed.

"You enjoying your stint in criminal law? I'm sure it's been quite a change from your corporate days."

"Yes, and yes."

"You know, I did six years with a big firm in Chicago. Couldn't stomach the gluttony. Good for you for getting out."

David didn't respond. How long would he have to endure this?

Mason didn't let David's lack of enthusiasm slow him down. "How're things going over at your little firm? What's it called again?"

"Gray and Adams."

"Heard you guys were having a little trouble with your lease."

David tried not to flinch. What the hell? Did Mason have something to do with the eviction notice? Did the man have that kind of immediate reach? David glanced over at Dana, who just stood there stoically, like she'd rather be anywhere else in the world right now.

"No trouble," David replied, keeping his cool. "Just a mix-up. Everything is going great at our firm. Couldn't be better, as a matter of fact."

"Glad to hear it. You ever handle a murder case, David?"

"I think you already know the answer to that."

"Right. Certainly not a death penalty case." Mason grinned, as if the thought of ending a man's life pleased him. "Well, if you need any guidance, I've asked Dana to help walk you through the various procedures. It can get complicated for a rookie. I don't want you to feel too overwhelmed."

"How nice of you," David said. "Let's talk about a plea deal."

Mason smiled wide, every tooth gleaming white. David wanted to grab the miniature football away from him, throw it so hard at the man's face that it knocked his perfect front teeth right out.

"There will be no deal offered to your client on this one," Mason said. "He brutally gunned down someone who worked inside our office. He did it with malice and without remorse. And while your client may have a bunch of his own wild conspiracy thoughts—none of which will play well in a courtroom, mind you—he was clearly competent enough to know exactly what he was doing."

"That's still debatable."

Mason's smile tightened. "Don't waste my time with psychiatrists, David. You won't get anywhere, and it'll only piss me off."

"Your mood is of no real concern to me."

"It should be. This can go a lot of different ways for you."

"Can I see the file now?"

Mason looked over at Dana, who handed David a manila envelope secured with a rubber band.

"What about the security video?" David asked.

"There's a flash drive inside the envelope," Dana explained. "It's all there, I promise. I copied everything myself."

David stood, already sick of dealing with Mason. "This has been fun. Thanks for your time."

"See you in court, kiddo."

FOURTEEN

David found a TV reporter who looked like he still belonged in high school waiting for him right outside the front door of his office building. The kid jumped off the steps upon seeing David approach. David recognized him from the local news channel. The reporter had short black hair plastered to his head and wore a white button-down shirt and khaki pants that were two sizes too big for him.

"Mr. Adams, my name's Theodore Billings—"

"I know who you are," David interrupted, sidestepping him. "I'm not interested."

"Come on, man. This case is major news. People want to know you."

David wondered if there was any advantage in putting himself in front of the camera right now. Mason's perfect smile was showcased in every other news clip.

"Do people want to know me? Or do you TV vultures just want to create an even bigger spectacle of the whole thing?"

"A lawyer calling a reporter a vulture? That's funny."

"What's in it for me?"

"The opportunity to shape your side of the story. Otherwise, people just speculate. In this case, I don't think speculation is a good thing for you. Just give me ten minutes."

"I'll think about it."

David shut the building door behind him and hustled up the stairs. Minutes later, he huddled with Thomas inside his front office. The DA's discovery file consisted of copies of the arresting officer's statement, a detailed account of their interview with the witness from Burnside's Tavern, and two other witness statements—both of whom reported seeing Rebel flee out of the alley and down the sidewalk. The two witnesses also mentioned seeing a couple of other people run out of the same alley right after the incident. Could one of them have seen what really happened? None of the three witness statements in the file claimed to have actually seen Rebel shoot Murphy, so David still had that going for him. The DA's file also contained photos that showed Murphy's dead body, which were difficult for him to view. Attached to a photo of the gun used in the attack, there was a ballistics report matching Rebel's prints to the gun. None of this surprised him, which was good; however, David had to admit seeing all the evidence compiled in one place felt overwhelming. No wonder Mason was acting so cocky—the jerk had good reason.

"Shall we look at the video?" Thomas asked.

"Not sure I want to see it, but here goes nothing."

Sticking the flash drive into his laptop, David pulled up the sidewalk security video. He could tell from the opening image that the camera was located above a building along Neches Street—the opposite end of the alley from where Rebel had run away and from where Murphy had parked his vehicle. As David pressed "Play," they huddled close to the laptop screen. The video was edited to a brief thirty seconds. Murphy immediately entered the screen from the right, which meant he was walking away from Sixth Street. He wore a white button-down shirt with the sleeves rolled up, no tie, and gray suit pants that matched the jacket in his car. Murphy was talking on his cell phone as he turned to enter the alley. Was he still on the phone when he was shot? A few other pedestrians strolled along the sidewalk on the video. Seconds later, a man wearing a green military-style jacket and a black knit cap also appeared and quickly entered the alley behind Murphy. Then the video abruptly ended.

David rewound the video and watched it again. He couldn't see the face of the man in the green jacket. He had tucked it down and out of view, almost as if he knew to hide it from any building security cameras. Was that possible? Or did David just want to believe it? The guy was about the same size as Rebel, which was not helpful. And the figure definitely seemed to be moving intentionally into the alley.

"You can't tell for sure it's Rebel," David stated.

"You also can't tell it's *not* Rebel," Thomas countered.

"True. But it at least keeps our defense alive."

"Our defense being what at this point? A theory that someone else wore the green jacket and black hat into the alley, shot and killed Luke Murphy, and then put the clothing items onto a blacked-out homeless guy?"

"Correct."

"Pretty far-fetched."

"But not impossible. We just have to create plausible doubt."

"All righty." Thomas sighed. "Where is this Dirty Dog Bar?"

Pulling up a map on his phone, David showed it to Thomas.

Thomas began pacing. "If Murphy stayed true to the scheduled meeting you found in his *stolen* day planner—which I wish I knew nothing about—he'd likely have just finished meeting with someone at this bar. Which meant he was probably cutting through the alley on his way back to his car."

"That's my running theory."

"So who is this mysterious KP?"

David shrugged. "Someone secretive enough for Murphy to keep their real name out of his day planner."

"You're starting to sound like our client with all of your conspiracies. It could be anyone, David. It could have no connection at all."

"And I'll cross it out as a possibility as soon as we can confirm that."

Thomas thumbed back through the file. "According to some of these witness statements, there were other people in the alley that night."

"The real killer could've been among them."

Thomas nodded. "We need to see if any security video from the opposite end of the alley exists."

"Doc is out there seeing what he can find from other bars."

"We need to check city cameras, too."

"How do we do that?"

"I'll look into it. I know a guy."

"Thanks. So you've never been to the Dirty Dog?"

Thomas shook his head. "Not my kind of place."

"It wasn't Murphy's kind of place, either."

"So what was he doing there?"

"I don't know. But hopefully I'm about to find out."

FIFTEEN

Everything David needed to know about the Dirty Dog could be found in the sign above the bar's entrance—a happy bulldog humping the leg of a surprised half-naked woman. Heavy-metal music blared as David entered, and groups of leather-vested and tattooed men banged around at the pool tables. Had KP chosen this meeting location? If so, why had this person wanted to meet here?

Grabbing an open stool at the main bar, David noticed two heavy-set, long-bearded men three barstools down give him a serious once-over. Although David had ditched the business suit, he still looked rather preppy for this place in his jeans, running shoes, and brown leather jacket.

A female bartender came over. Wearing a white tank top that showcased her muscle-bound arms, which were completely covered in tattoos, she looked like she could easily break David in half. Even the short, spiky pink hair looked tough.

"What can I get you, hon?" she asked.

"Coors Light," David said.

She stepped a few paces down, filled him a tall glass, brought it back over.

"Nice place," David mentioned.

"Tell that to your face," the bartender suggested, smiling.

He matched her smile, tried to relax a bit, took a drink of the beer.

"I'm David."

"I'm single," she replied, winking. "But you can call me Blaze."

"Good to meet you. Were you working here two nights ago?"

"Depends. Why do you want to know?"

"You hear about the prosecutor who got murdered a block over?"

"Sure. Everyone was talking about it."

"I think he was in your bar a few minutes before he was killed."

She eyeballed him. "You a cop?"

"No, I'm a lawyer."

She grinned. "Even worse."

He laughed, took another drink.

She peered down the bar toward the two huge men on the stools. "Those guys don't like lawyers too much, so don't tell anyone in here what you do, okay?"

"Can't say I blame them."

"But you're cute," she said. "I'll protect you."

"I appreciate that."

David welcomed the flirting. It meant she'd probably be helpful.

"You haven't been in here before, have you?" she said.

"First time."

"Then that beer is on me, hon."

"Thanks. About my question . . ."

"Yeah, I'm here every night. Except when I'm fighting."

"Fighting?"

"I do the MMA circuit."

"Oh, impressive." David knew that stood for *mixed martial arts*, a violent full-contact combat sport. Blaze really could protect him from the bikers.

"You got a picture of the guy?"

David pulled out his phone, showed her a photo of Murphy.

"Yeah, I remember him. He was here." She pointed. "They were sitting down at the far end of the bar over there."

"They?"

"He was with a woman."

"Any chance you got her name?"

She shook her head. "Nah, but she was an attractive girl. Pretty eyes. Nice black hair, although most of it was tucked under a ball cap. An Astros cap, because I remember making a joke with her about my Dodgers."

David wondered if it could be the same woman who approached him outside the county jail last night. He looked above the bar by the TVs. "Any security cameras in here?"

She laughed. "You kidding? Believe me, both the owner and our customers want no evidence of what happens in this place every night."

"You ever seen either of them in here before?"

"Can't say for sure. But they seemed to be into each other."

"Really?"

"They were snuggled up together real good." She shrugged. "They weren't here for too long."

"They leave together?"

"Don't recall, hon, sorry."

David glanced down toward the end of the bar, tried to imagine Murphy sitting with an attractive woman who wasn't his wife. Could he have been having an affair? That didn't seem possible. Murphy was such a stable family guy. He never even joked about other girls. If it wasn't an affair, what was it?

David dropped cash on the bar. "I appreciate your help, Blaze."

"Leaving already?"

"I don't think this is the place for preppy lawyers. If I stay much longer, those guys might try to use me as a pool stick."

"How about you come watch me fight sometime? I can get you seats so close, you might get blood on your shoes."

David forced a smile. Watching blood splatter was not really his cup of tea.

"That's quite the offer," he said, politely sidestepping the invite.

"You know where to find me, cutie."

SIXTEEN

The next morning, David picked up his old truck from the auto shop—where he'd dropped $500 he barely had to get the alternator replaced—and then drove out to Smithville, a small town of several thousand an hour east of Austin. Doc had managed to connect some dots through different street friends and somehow tracked down Rebel's ex-wife. David thought it might be good to get a better perspective on his client's past, although Doc had warned him that the ex-wife seemed a bit hostile over the phone. Using his map app to guide him, David followed three different long dirt roads. The pin in the map finally settled him at Pine Tree Trailer Park, a cluster of rather run-down RVs and trailers.

David slowly drove the dusty circle past all the trailers. Several chickens were running loose on the property. There were various cars parked here and there, some of which looked like they'd probably never start up again. Tires were missing, hoods popped open, tall grass growing around several of them. Marcy North's trailer was located in the back corner of the property. The RV looked to be in decent shape, with the green space all around it properly maintained. A late-model white Kia Sorrento was sitting out front, caked in dust. David parked in front of the trailer and eased up the steps to a small wooden deck that held two plastic chairs surrounded by several potted flowers. There was an ashtray on a small table that was overflowing with cigarette butts.

He knocked on the door, waited. It was going to be interesting to find out what kind of woman was once married to his client. According to Rebel, the marriage had ended about five years ago. Marcy had never remarried. His ex-wife had kept his surname for some reason.

Hearing noise inside, David took a small step back. The lock released, the door cracked, and then a woman with frizzy bleached-blonde hair appeared in the doorway.

"You that damn lawyer?" she asked.

"Yes, ma'am. David Adams."

"Hold on a sec."

Seconds later, Marcy reappeared and stepped outside with him onto the deck. Behind her inside the trailer, David noticed a small boy sitting on the worn carpet playing video games on a TV. The boy looked up at him. He was the spitting image of Rebel. Same clear blue eyes and long hair. Marcy closed the trailer door. She wore a sleeveless black Iron Maiden T-shirt and cutoff blue-jean shorts. She was skinny and yellowed, as if years of smoking several packs a day had gradually altered her skin color. Still, David could tell she had been a beauty at one point.

"I appreciate you agreeing to see me," David said.

She lit up a cigarette, dropped into one of the plastic chairs. "Got nothing better to do today, anyway."

"Mind if I sit?" David asked.

"Free country."

David eased down into the chair next to Marcy, readjusted his position so as to not get caught in the direct crosshairs of her puffing.

"So that idiot finally did it, huh?" she said, taking a long drag. "I knew it would happen someday. Just a matter of time before he actually killed a man."

"Why do you say that?"

"Rebel was a loose cannon from the day I met him. Hell, he used to take a swing at every damn guy who even looked twice at me at the bars. Got his ass kicked too many times to count." She grinned, puffed. "'Course, he kicked a lot of ass, too, believe me. Used to find it kind of sweet."

"When was the last time you saw Rebel?"

"Not since he left. Haven't heard a single word from him in over five years. You'd think he'd come around here and there at least to see his son. But he don't. Not even a phone call. Junior is better off without him, anyway."

"How long were you guys married?"

"Two of the lousiest years of my life."

"Was Rebel physically violent with you?"

She shook her head. "Nah, just a yeller. He never touched me. I was his queen."

"So why did the marriage end?"

"He just kept getting worse until I couldn't take it anymore."

"Worse, how?"

"Always talking about these make-believe people who were after him. The stupid CIA this and that. He was so obsessed with it that he'd never shut up. Drove me freaking crazy. And he'd never let us stay anywhere for too long, either. He kept wanting to move us every damn month. Over and over again. I'd finally had enough and told him I wasn't going anywhere no more. That's when I woke up one night, and Junior was gone. Rebel had taken him. I tracked them down outside Texarkana at his uncle's place. That's when it was over for me. You try to take my kid, you lucky to still be breathing."

"Did he talk about people being after him from the beginning?"

She pondered that. "Here and there, but I always just thought he was trying to be silly. I never took him too serious. But it quickly grew worse."

"Did he ever seek medical help?"

She looked over at him with a wrinkled brow. "Like a shrink? Hell no! That man was as stubborn as a mule. Hell, he never thought anything was wrong with him. We were all the crazy ones."

"Rebel told me he suffers from blackouts."

"You mean his stupid 'spells'?"

"Right. Is it true?"

She took another long drag, finished off that cigarette, shoved it into the crowded ashtray. "Who the hell knows for sure? Sometimes I'd find out he'd been with another woman, but he would try to tell me that he'd had a 'spell' and couldn't remember anything."

"You think he was making them up?"

Marcy lit up another cigarette, began puffing again. "Nah, I think some of them were real. I found him passed out behind a bar a few times, and it wasn't from drinking too much. He'd just gotten there, but he was already out cold. When I'd wake him up, he couldn't even tell me how he'd ended up there. Although it started to follow a bit of a pattern, I think."

"What kind of pattern?"

"It usually happened right after Rebel had done something violent. Like pick a fight with someone. Had a girlfriend once tell me she watched it happen. Rebel hit a man over the head with a bottle, walked outside, sat down in the dirt by his truck, leaned up against the tire, and just drifted off for a good while."

"You really think he could kill a man?"

She took a moment. "Hell, I don't know."

David eased back in his chair, thinking about what she'd just said about how violence usually preceded the blackouts. It did not bode well for his client's defense. If the pattern held true, what violent thing had Rebel just done that would've made him black out? Shoot a man?

"Anything else you can think of that might help, Marcy?"

She shrugged. "Not really. I've got an old box of Rebel's crap. Tell him I'm going to burn it if he doesn't come back to get it soon."

"I can bring it to him, if you want."

"Sure. I'm sick of it taking up closet space."

Marcy went inside the trailer for a few minutes and then returned with a worn bankers box with a lid on it. On the outside, she'd scribbled the word *IDIOT* in black marker.

"I'm surprised he even hired you," Marcy said. "Rebel hates lawyers."

"Most people do."

"What's going to happen to him?"

"Too soon to know. We'll go to trial in a few months. I'm going to do my best to represent him in the court of law."

"They really going to put him to death if you lose?"

"It's still early. But that's what they're saying."

Marcy lit up again. "I don't want to see him die, Mr. Adams. Don't tell him nothing, but I still love him. Even if he's crazy."

Leaving the trailer park, David pulled over at a nearby gas station and began sorting through the contents of the dusty bankers box. There were a couple of shiny silver cowboy belt buckles, where it looked like Rebel might have won some bull-riding contests during his youth. Two framed photographs of his client as a small boy with probably his mother—Rebel sitting in her lap at Christmastime, and both of them on a merry-go-round at an amusement park. There was a pair of black cowboy boots. Branded inside one of the boots was the name *Sandy North*. Rebel's father's boots. Searching further, David found paperback copies of several classics: Steinbeck's *Of Mice and Men*, Faulkner's *The Sound and the Fury*, and Hemingway's *For Whom the Bell Tolls*. There was a faded blue football jersey with an *18* on the front and back.

In the bottom of the box, David pulled out an accordion file bound with a rubber band. In the very front were dozens of newspaper clippings about the death of Osama bin Laden—something Rebel had brought up the first time they'd met. The clippings were from both American and Russian publications. David couldn't read the Russian articles. Could Rebel? His client had certainly highlighted and circled a lot of the contents of the Russian articles. Next, David opened a spiral notebook filled with pages upon pages of scribbled notes all about the operation that had found the notorious terrorist. There were all kinds of random writings and drawings about the Iraqis, the Chinese, the Russians, the Pakistanis, and the CIA, with things circled here and there, and arrows drawn everywhere. None of it made any sense to David.

Continuing to search the file, David discovered an envelope with a copy of Rebel's official military personnel file, including his health and service records. Nothing in his health records indicated he displayed any manic behavior as a young man. His health looked solid. His service record showed he was in the marines from 2001 to 2005 and had served in Iraq.

David's phone buzzed with a new text message from Thomas.

Reading it, David cursed out loud. His partner said there was a last-minute change of location for their scheduled meeting to discuss the recent eviction notice with the new building owners. The ownership group wanted them to meet with their lawyer instead, which was never a good sign.

That wasn't what had rattled David—it was the name of the damn lawyer.

William Tidmore of Hunter & Kellerman.

SEVENTEEN

David met Thomas in the lobby of the Frost Bank Tower.

"Is this for real?" David asked. "Tidmore?"

"It's real, I'm afraid. You ready to beg forgiveness?"

"I think I'd rather work out of my truck than have to suck up to Tidmore."

"Not me. So just keep your cool, and let me handle it."

They traveled up the elevator to the twenty-sixth floor, where they stepped into the familiar grand lobby of the richest law firm in town. A dozen different emotions hit David all at once. It was hard to believe that not even a year had passed since he'd walked into this firm for the first time, the newest member of an elite group of lawyers who were all fabulously wealthy. Not much had changed. The lobby rugs and artwork were still fancy. The floors shone. The place just smelled like money. At one point, he'd loved that smell—now it made him a bit queasy. They checked in with the receptionist and then took a seat on two plush leather couches. It felt strange to be sitting there as a guest. Eight months ago, he'd been the toast of this place. A rookie who had just broken the firm's long-standing one-month billing record. On the fast track to partner. Now he was sleeping on a sofa because he couldn't afford rent anywhere.

"How'd it go with the ex-wife?" Thomas asked.

"Let's just say we won't be putting her on the stand."

David explained Marcy's view of their client's spells.

"Violence, followed by blackouts," Thomas repeated. "Let's hope Mason doesn't go looking for Marcy."

"Any luck yet with getting access to city security cameras?"

"Not yet. I feel like I'm getting the runaround. I keep getting passed off to others, who won't call me back. But I'll keep pressing. Doc called a few minutes ago, said he was able to get another camera view he thought might be helpful. He's at the office, waiting for us to get back."

The receptionist came over. "Mr. Tidmore is ready for you."

Trailing the receptionist, David took a hallway path he'd traveled a thousand times last year over to the main conference room, passing by several associate offices in the process. None of his former colleagues even looked up from their desks. Their tired faces and glazed-over eyes were all buried in their laptops or in piles of paperwork. A few of the assistants and paralegals said hello as they made their way down the hallway.

The conference room had a huge glass wall, and David noticed Tidmore standing inside, wearing a black suit, already looking so damn smug. Opening the glass door, the receptionist led them into the room. Tidmore walked over to greet them, shaking Thomas's hand first. When he stuck out his hand for David, Tidmore gave him the familiar cocky grin.

"Good to see you, pal," Tidmore said, clearly enjoying this moment. "Wish it were under better circumstances."

"I bet."

They all sat down around the conference table.

"Thanks for meeting with us," Thomas began, ever the diplomat. "Obviously, we received the notice from the new building owners. I think it's just a big misunderstanding, and we would like to sort this all out."

"Not sure that's possible," Tidmore replied. "My client just spent five point seven million dollars to purchase your building, so they're taking a hard look at all of the current lease agreements and—"

"Just cut to the chase, Tidmore," David interrupted. "What's this about?"

Tidmore slid over a folder. "Here's a copy of your lease. Take a look at the highlighted section. It specifically states that a tenant must not operate a business in a way that negatively impacts other building tenants. Or their lease will be subject to termination."

"How're we doing that?" Thomas questioned. "We're a law firm."

"Well, sort of," Tidmore mocked. "It's not necessarily the nature of your business that's the problem here. It's your clientele, to be frank."

David was surprised this wasn't about his sleeping at the office. "You want to throw us out of the building because some of our clients wear dirty clothes?"

"*And* they smell really bad," Tidmore added. "Like it or not, you guys have a bunch of clients that are disruptive to the other tenants in the building. We've received dozens of complaints."

"Which other tenants?" David said.

"I'm not at liberty to say," Tidmore replied.

"Because it's BS, and you know it," David countered. "This is discrimination."

"How do we make this right, William?" Thomas asked, staying calm.

"You can't. They want you out by the end of the month."

"That's in *seventeen* days," Thomas said.

"Correct," Tidmore replied. "Better get to packing."

David felt a righteous anger bubbling up inside him. "We'll sue your ass."

"Bring it on," Tidmore said, flashing his perfect teeth.

David's face flushed red, but he was able to hold his rage back. It was clear that Tidmore hoped to get a rise out of him. He wasn't going to allow the jerk the pleasure, even though everything inside of him wanted to unload on the guy.

Back in the elevator, David said, "I'm serious. We should sue."

"And take on Hunter and Kellerman?" Thomas asked.

"Why not?"

"Because we have about three hundred dollars left in our bank account. They probably spend that on coffee creamer every day."

EIGHTEEN

Back at the office, David huddled with Thomas and Doc around his TV to watch the new security-camera video that Doc had gotten ahold of. Doc mentioned that he'd visited over a dozen bars before finding someone who was willing to play along. Most establishments weren't all that interested in sharing anything with him outside of a court order—something David would have to consider pursuing if they couldn't find what they needed down their current path.

"Which bar?" David asked Doc.

"Coyote Ugly. Corner of Sixth and Neches."

"How'd you get it?" Thomas questioned him.

"Slipped the bartender forty bucks. He swore he knew how to operate the cameras from the back room and would get what I wanted when the manager stepped out."

"Good work, Doc," David said.

Doc shrugged. "Bartender said this particular shot is aimed down the sidewalk in the direction we wanted."

Loading the video drive onto his laptop, David pulled it up onto the TV for everyone to see. The bartender was right—the camera view was aimed down the sidewalk away from Sixth Street and toward the correct alley. The same shot of the alley as the DA's video but from a different direction. Because the bartender had downloaded several hours of footage from the night in question, David quickly fast-forwarded it to the appropriate time stamp, then let it play out in front of them.

"There he is," Thomas said, pointing at the screen.

Murphy walked into view, his back to the camera. But it was easy for David to tell it was Murphy. He recognized the familiar gait and had already memorized the footage from the other security video. While talking on his phone, Murphy dipped into the alley and disappeared from view. Moments later, the mysterious man in the green military jacket and black knit cap appeared, just like in the other video. David still couldn't get a look at the man's face with his full back to the camera. He tried to examine any mannerisms that might suggest it was someone other than his client. The man was around the same height and build. The black knit cap completely covered whatever hair the guy had on his head. David rewound the video, and they all watched it closely again.

Thomas cursed. "You can't tell a thing."

David sat on the edge of his desk, feeling deflated, while the video continued to play out on the TV screen. "Wait a sec . . ."

A few seconds after the man in the green jacket and black hat had entered the alley, a second person appeared in the shot wearing jeans, a gray hoodie, and a blue ball cap. This person also entered the alley from the same direction. David had not gotten this sequence from the other footage—the DA's video cut off before this person entered the scene. Why? Not ten seconds later, the same person in the ball cap and hoodie came scrambling back out, looking panicked, and took off running out of view. Rewinding the video yet again, David paused it just as this new person's face was in clear view of the security camera. A woman in her midtwenties, black hair poking out of the back of an Astros ball cap. It had to be the woman who was with Murphy at Dirty Dog just minutes earlier. Staring at the screen, David recognized her as the same woman who had stepped out of the shadows in front of him at the county jail the other night. Her words to him echoed anew in his mind.

There's more to the story.

NINETEEN

David immediately exchanged texts with Dana, who was having lunch at the Roaring Fork with two colleagues just up the street from his office. He wanted to talk with her right away. He entered the restaurant and spotted her at a table in the corner. She noticed him, excused herself, and they slipped off together down a quiet hallway near the restrooms where they could talk in private.

"What's so urgent?" Dana asked.

"*This,*" David replied, holding up his phone.

He played the new video for Dana, showing her the footage of the woman in the ball cap and gray hoodie.

"Where'd you get this?" she asked, eyebrows raised.

"Doesn't matter. Why is *this* not on the DA's video?"

"I don't know."

"You're telling me this is the first you've seen of it?"

"Yes."

"Come on, Dana. Why is the DA's video edited?"

Her forehead bunched. "You think I'm lying to you, David?"

"I don't know, but *something's* going on here."

"I've never seen this part," Dana assured him.

"Has Mason?"

"How the hell am I supposed to know that?"

"You work with him."

"I work *for* him," she clarified. "There's a difference. And you and I both know I'm only on this case because he's trying to mess with you. Seems to be working, if you ask me. You're acting a little paranoid."

"Okay, I'm sorry. But what's the source of the DA's video?"

"A city camera, I think."

David shook his head. "Funny, Dana, no one with the city will even respond to any of *our* requests for footage. We keep getting the runaround."

"Careful with your accusations, okay? Not everything is a government conspiracy. Mason may be an ass, but I've never known him to be unethical. There's probably nothing to it. This footage could be nothing more than some random woman who walked into the alley and saw your client shoot Murphy. Hell, she might help our case and not harm it. I think you need to calm down, take a step back into reality, and stop drinking from your client's crazy Kool-Aid cup."

"Except this woman had just met with Murphy at a bar a half block away."

"How do you know that?"

"According to a bartender at the Dirty Dog, Murphy was sitting closely with this very same woman just a few minutes before he was killed. Do you recognize her?"

"Play it again."

Replaying the video, he paused it with the woman's face in full view. Black hair, ball cap, pretty eyes.

"I don't know her," Dana insisted. "Maybe they were just flirting. People do that in bars. Murphy was a good-looking guy."

"He went to the bar specifically to meet her, Dana."

She tilted her head. "Are you sure?"

"He wrote it down in his day planner."

"Where'd you get his day planner?"

"You don't want to know."

"You're right, I don't. He wrote down her name?"

"No, only the initials *KP*. But this same woman approached me two nights ago outside the county jail, right after I'd gotten through meeting with Rebel. She asked me if I was representing the guy who was accused of murdering the prosecutor. She claimed there was more to the story. But she got spooked and took off before I could get anything more out of her. I didn't take her too seriously—until now."

Dana crossed her arms, brow furrowed. "Do you think Murphy could have been having an affair?"

"I'd had that initial thought. But then I'd never even heard him talk about another woman, even in joking terms. From everything I knew about Murphy, the guy was a faithful oak."

"You're right. I made a pass at him once at a law school party. He didn't even entertain it for a moment."

David's mouth dropped open. He'd never heard that story. "Damn, Dana."

"Not my best moment, okay? But me and tequila aren't friends."

"Not to mention Murphy wouldn't write down a meeting for a fling in his day planner, right? That would be stupid."

"So who is she?"

David shrugged. "Doc cross-checked the contacts in Murphy's day planner, but we can't find *anyone* who matches up with KP."

"This could still be nothing."

"Or it could be *everything*. Will you at least look into it for me? Check Murphy's files, his work contacts, see if you can find a connection? And while you're at it, find out why the hell your video cut this woman completely out."

She frowned at him. "Do I need to remind you that we're not on the same team here?"

"When did finding the truth begin to have teams?"

"When the legal system was created. Don't be naive. I have a job to do here. And you're pushing me to step into dangerous territory."

"You're right. I'm sorry. I don't mean to put you in a bad spot. But what if Murphy's killer is still out there? What if he was involved in something that got him killed? Murphy *always* had your back. Don't you owe it to him to look into this?"

Dana sighed. "Send me this video. I'll see what I can find out."

TWENTY

David found Curly waiting for him, along with another man, in a parking lot under I-35 later that afternoon. The busy interstate overhead rumbled loudly with the steady passage of heavy 18-wheelers. Curly wore the same denim jacket, jeans, and work boots that he'd had on nearly every day since David had first met him at the Camp last year. Even with the extended wear, the clothes were clean, in good shape, and absent from the usual odors of the streets. The boys at the Camp used to regularly wash their clothes with the same makeshift rain bucket system they'd also used for showering. When their camp was destroyed, they'd all had to scramble to make temporary homes in other parts of the city.

Some of the guys were really struggling. Curly had told him that more than missing the conveniences of the Camp—like the showers, kitchen, and chapel—they mostly missed the community. They were stronger together. David understood. There had been something magical about a group of men of all ages, races, and creeds, sitting around a campfire sharing their lives with each other in such an open and honest way. That's why developing Benny's village was so important to him.

Curly introduced him to the other man. "Shep, this is Moses. He said he hangs with Rebel here and there."

David shook the man's dirty hand. Moses had a long, unkempt gray beard, a trucker cap, and wore jeans and a white T-shirt that were both soaked in stains and reeked something awful. His tennis shoes had big holes in both fronts, showing the man's mangled and bloodied toes.

"Good to meet you, Moses."

Moses just nodded.

"How do you know Rebel?" David asked.

"Met him a few years back. Couple of guys tried to rob me behind the Broken Spoke one night. Rebel put one of them down with a swing of the fist and chased the other off. We kinda been running buddies ever since."

"I'd heard Rebel didn't have too many friends."

"He don't. Got too much of a temper. But I don't talk much, you see. I think he likes that, 'cause that man won't ever stop talking."

"Sounds about right."

Curly interjected. "Tell him what you told me, Moses. About the other night."

"You were with Rebel the night of the murder?" David asked.

Moses nodded, spit at the pavement. "We was drinking and shooting pool over at the Buffalo, like we do sometimes."

"Buffalo Billiards?"

Another nod of the head. David knew the pool hall was on Sixth, right around the corner from where Murphy was killed.

"Around what time?" he asked Moses.

Moses shrugged. "Time don't mean too much to me, mister. It was night and packed, so must've been getting kinda late. Anyways, Rebel was going on and on about things, like he usually does, getting himself all worked up. Then he put his stick down on the table, right in the middle of our game, says to me that he's got to go somewhere. I asked him why, since we usually drink and play until the place closes down—especially when Rebel has rounded up a bit of extra cash somehow. He tells me he's got to go settle a score with someone."

"A score? With who?"

"Hell if I know. He always talked that way. But this felt a little different."

"Why?"

"He'd been keeping an eye on the clock. Like he had to be somewhere at a certain time or something."

"He never mentioned any names?"

Another small shrug. "Didn't pay much attention to most of what he said. It was always the Russians this, the CIA that."

"Was Rebel wearing a green jacket and a black knit cap that night?"

Moses shook his head, spat again. "Nah, he was wearing one of them Western pearl snap shirts. Think he has two or three of them. Nice shirts. He says he got them from Clint Eastwood out in LA."

"You ever seen Rebel with a gun?"

"Nope. He hates guns. I think it has to do with his time in the marines or something." Moses smiled, showing a severe case of stained teeth. "He also hates wearing hats. Says it would be a sin to cover up his beautiful hair."

"You left the pool hall together?" David asked.

Moses nodded. "No reason for me to stay. I never got more than two bucks to my name. I came back over here to hit the hay."

David looked over, noticed a tightly wound sleeping bag on the pavement next to a black backpack. All the man's worldly possessions.

"Where did Rebel get his money?" David asked.

"Beats me. But he always seems to have a little extra cash on him."

"He sell drugs?"

"Nah, that ain't Rebel."

"You ever seen him black out?"

"Whatcha mean?"

"Like become disoriented and pass out for a few minutes."

"Only after drinking too much. But he'd be out all night."

"You know where Rebel stays at night?"

"Nah, he don't like company. If he wants to play pool, he knows how to find me. That's about it."

David thanked Moses for the information, watched the man get his stuff and wander off. Then he and Curly discussed the situation.

"What do you think, Shep?" Curly asked.

"I don't like the sound of it."

"You think Moses is lying?"

"No, I don't. But sounds like Rebel was going somewhere with the intent to harm someone in particular."

"Sure does."

David sighed. He kept trying to find an opening that led him down a path toward Rebel's actual innocence. But so far everyone they talked with—Marcy and now Moses—had told credible stories that made it hard to believe.

"I'll keep checking around," Curly said. "See who else I can round up."

"Thanks, Curly. Hey, you get any work over at that construction site?"

Curly possessed some good carpentry skills, so he was usually able to find odd jobs here and there. Just enough work to barely keep his feet beneath him. Most of David's street friends lived day to day—or even hour to hour. A stressful path of survival that David felt like he was beginning to better understand as the money in his own bank account continued to dwindle down to nothing.

"They throwing me a few hours here and there. Not much. But enough for a couple of meals, some change for the Laundromat. But I ain't complaining, you know. Some of the boys got it way worse than me out here."

Although David's street friends never had much, they rarely complained about it. He admired that. His former colleagues over at Hunter & Kellerman had damn near everything but never seemed to stop whining about wanting more.

David's phone buzzed in his pocket. Staring at the text message on his screen, he didn't recognize the random phone number. He found only a link in the text message to a news article from the *Austin American-Statesman*. Clicking on the link, he skimmed a story in the newspaper from a few days ago about the fatal shooting of a young man in a parking lot outside a local Tejano nightclub. Police suspected a drug deal. David had no idea who or why someone would send him such a link. He replied with three question marks, but no response came back. So he shrugged it off. His clients would often pass out his phone number to other friends on the streets. It wasn't odd for David to receive random text messages from anonymous phone numbers.

"Do me a favor, Curly," David said. "Bring Moses by the office tomorrow. We need to get him some new socks and shoes before he loses a couple of his toes."

"You got it, Shep."

TWENTY-ONE

Late that afternoon, David got a call that Shifty had found Rebel's dog and his camp. As the sun was setting on the day, David met the old man with the missing two front teeth and patchy white hair under an overpass near the running trail on the south side of Lady Bird Lake. Shifty was holding the small dog, Sandy, which looked like some version of a Yorkshire terrier. David knew his client would be relieved to hear that his beloved mutt had managed to survive without him.

Following Shifty, David cut through a narrow path off the main trail, climbed over a short concrete wall, until they made their way up into the darkest recesses of the overpass. David doubted many people would find their way up here. Rebel probably liked the solitude and the fact that no one would likely steal his possessions while he was away. Theft was commonplace among his street friends, which is why so many of them carried, pushed, or pulled everything they owned everywhere they went.

David found a gray backpack and a rolled-up green sleeping bag among an assortment of empty beer cans and some random trash. Next to it were two empty silver dog bowls.

"How do you know this is his stuff?" David asked Shifty.

"Check the dog tags on the bag."

Kneeling, David found official metal military tags on a chain that were looped through a strap of the backpack: *North, Roger Eugene.*

"Elvis talked to a guy who thought he saw Rebel up here the other day," Shifty said. "Sure enough, when I came walking up here, this little guy started barking his head off. I recognized that yapping right away."

"Good work, Shifty."

The backpack looked rather new. David unzipped the front pocket. Inside, he found two packs of Marlboro cigarettes, a couple of lighters, two packages of peanut butter crackers, and a wad of rolled-up cash secured with a rubber band. David pulled out the cash, began counting it, which made the dog growl at him.

"Easy there," Shifty told the dog. "We're not stealing anything."

David calculated $600. How did Rebel have that much money on him? It was highly unusual for his street friends to have a roll of cash. Moses had mentioned earlier that Rebel always seemed to have a little extra cash. So where did he get it?

Checking the second pocket, David found a large Ziploc bag that contained a toothbrush and toothpaste, a stick of deodorant, a travel-size shampoo, a couple of bars of soap, a can of shaving cream, and several razors that were still in their new packages. He also found a prescription pill bottle for something called Clozaril. The bottle was about half-full.

"What's that, Shep?" Shifty asked.

"Not sure."

On his phone, David did a quick Google search. The drug was used to treat schizophrenia. The prescription was under Rebel's real name and written nine months ago by a Dr. M. Wong in Tucson. David did another quick search and found that Dr. Wong was legitimate. Rebel had apparently been to a doctor about his condition after all.

"Rebel doing drugs?" Shifty asked.

"Doctor prescribed," David clarified. "Supposed to help keep him stable."

"Drugs don't do that," Shifty said with a toothless smile. "The only thing that can do that is the Holy Ghost."

Shifty had a joy about him that had always made David feel good. Whether it was the Holy Ghost or something else, Shifty had managed to overcome a difficult road. He'd once been a truck driver from Alabama. Came home from a road trip and found his wife in bed with another man. Shifty said he lost his mind and put the man in the hospital with a broken jaw, a cracked skull, several broken ribs, and a punctured lung. It was hard to imagine the frail old man in front of him doing so much damage to another human being. The injured guy recovered, but Shifty didn't. After serving sixty days' jail time, he hit the bottle even harder, wrecked his company's truck, destroyed all the valuables he was carrying, and got fired. Thus began his drifting days. The out-of-control boozing continued for nearly two decades and kept him wandering from town to town just to survive. The old man found refuge with the boys at the Camp three years ago and finally got sober. It changed his entire life. Shifty had spent the past couple of years helping others on the street also get clean. He claimed it was his life purpose, his second chance, and he liked to keep a running tally of the number of street friends he'd helped get into treatment centers.

"What's your number today, Shifty?" David asked him.

Another big smile. "Thirty-two."

"That's three more since the last time I asked you."

"Yessir! And I'm real close with two others. Pray for Willy and Janet."

"Will do."

David continued his search of the second pocket, finding paperback copies of *The Catcher in the Rye* and *To Kill a Mockingbird*. He never took Rebel for a reader of the classics—or any books, for that matter—but he'd found similar books in the box the ex-wife had given him.

Finding a leather-bound Bible in the pocket, David opened it and read an inscription written on the first page.

My prayers are with you. —Benny

Seeing Benny's familiar messy handwriting nearly made David tear up. He quickly flipped through the Bible and found that dozens of the pages had been marked with a pencil or pen, where it looked like Rebel had either circled or underlined different passages and even made notes in the margins. It surprised David that the man sitting in jail had so thoroughly engaged with the Scriptures.

In the bigger section of the backpack, David mostly found clothes. As Moses had suggested earlier, Rebel owned a few long-sleeve button-down Western-style shirts, all with fancy pearl snaps. Two clean white undershirts. A couple of pairs of underwear and socks. A black raincoat. Several plastic bottles of water were in the bigger section. There was also a small bag of dog food. David poured a bowl full for Sandy and filled up the other silver bowl with a bottle of the water. Shifty set down the dog, who raced over and immediately began devouring the food.

"Hungry mutt," Shifty said.

Finishing off his backpack search, David found a pair of Wrangler jeans. He stuck his hands in all the pockets, pulled out a couple of receipts from various stores, as well as a few business cards. The first card was for an auto shop on South Congress. The second was a pawnshop on Riverside.

The third card was like a sudden punch to the jaw.

Luke E. Murphy, Assistant District Attorney, Travis County

TWENTY-TWO

David paced in a tight circle around the table in the private jail room, waiting for his client to arrive. His mind was spinning sideways. Rebel had Murphy's business card. Had he lied to him about *everything*? A jail deputy finally led his client into the room. Rebel looked pleased to see him, a small grin on his face, an easygoing demeanor about him. Was his client pleased because he knew he'd managed to play his own lawyer? The deputy unfastened Rebel's handcuffs and left them alone. David dropped in the chair opposite Rebel, immediately pulled out Murphy's business card, and placed it on the table in front of his client.

"What the hell is this?" David asked, pointing at the card.

"Good to see you, too, Lawyer."

"Just answer my question, Rebel."

Rebel glanced at the card, eyes squinting, shrugged. "Why you acting so pissy all of a sudden?"

"Because you're lying to me."

"I ain't lying to you."

"I found this in your backpack."

Rebel perked up, eyes flashing. "You find my dog?"

"Yes, but—"

Rebel interrupted him. "He hurt? He hungry? Did anyone mess with him?"

"The dog is just fine, okay?"

"Where is he?"

"Back at my office. Can you forget about your damn dog for just a second? You told me you didn't know Murphy. You said it right to my face."

"I don't," Rebel insisted, nodding at the card. "That ain't mine."

"Come on, Rebel, stop it already. It was inside your blue jeans pocket."

"I ain't never seen it before."

David's frustration began to boil over. "So, what, now you're telling me someone planted it there? It took us two days to find your hideaway camp. But now you're trying to tell me someone else waltzed right up there, unzipped your backpack, and dropped this business card inside your pocket?"

"I don't know how it got there. Stop calling me a liar."

"Were you going to settle a score with Murphy the other night?"

"What . . . ?"

"I spoke with your buddy Moses. He said you bolted early on him that night, saying you had to go *settle a score* with someone."

"Moses said that?" Rebel asked, looking confused.

"Was it Murphy? Was he that someone?"

Rebel stared at his calloused hands, as if trying to think hard about it. "I don't . . . I don't know. But I do remember being at the pool hall with Moses."

David carefully watched his client. If he were in the middle of an ongoing charade, then Rebel was a damn fine actor. Still, David couldn't be sure, so he wanted to push at him from every angle. He had to get to the truth already.

"Your ex-wife says you usually had these blackout spells right after you were engaged in a violent incident. Like a bar fight."

Rebel's eyes were slits. "You talked to my ex?"

"Yes. Is that what happened? You shot Murphy and *then* blacked out?"

"I don't want you talking to that woman anymore!"

"Look, Rebel, *everything* is pointing right at you. My whole case was built on wrong place, wrong time." He put his finger on the business card. "But then I find this in your things. I can't defend you if you won't even tell me how this ended up in your backpack."

"Wait a second," Rebel said, as if something had crystallized for him. "I see what's going on here. They finally got to you, too, didn't they?"

"What are you talking about?"

"CIA flipped you against me."

David sighed. "Please stop already."

But Rebel didn't stop. "You wearing a wire right now? Are they listening to us?"

David put his face down into his hands, shook his head. Under his breath, he muttered, "Crazy."

Rebel heard it and was immediately up out of his chair, hurling himself across the table at David, his strong hands clutching him around his neck. David's chair flipped over backward, tumbling them both to the floor. Rebel was on top of him in a flash, the wildest look David had ever seen running through the man's eyes.

"I didn't do it, Lawyer!" Rebel yelled, hands still around David's neck.

"Rebel . . . please . . . stop . . . ," David managed, feeling the oxygen beginning to cut off.

"I didn't do it!" Rebel repeated, squeezing even harder.

The door to the room flung wide-open. Within seconds, three deputies were inside, grabbing Rebel from behind, yanking him off David, who immediately gasped for breath. The deputies pinned Rebel to the floor, slamming his client's head hard, and then they dragged him kicking and screaming out of the room.

Rebel's voice echoed in the hallways. "I didn't do it!"

TWENTY-THREE

David wandered the streets that night. He wanted to give himself a chance to clear his head, to think, and to figure out his next move. If he turned over Luke Murphy's business card to Mason—which he would eventually have to do as part of case discovery—it would seal his client's fate. David could offer a jury no plausible explanation for why it had been in his client's belongings. Was he supposed to claim someone else had planted it there? Surely he'd come off looking as foolish as his client.

Feeling stuck, David walked several blocks away from his office and made his way down Congress Avenue toward the river. He hoped Rebel was okay. The deputies had been rough on him. David felt terrible about that, especially because the whole incident was his fault. He should have never provoked his client. Hands in his jacket pockets, David strolled past the front entrance of the palatial fifty-six-story Austonian, where he used to live. He paused and watched as a sharply dressed man and woman exited the building together and climbed into a shiny Mercedes sedan a valet had waiting for them along the curb. Damn, they sure looked happy. Had he been that happy eight months ago? He already knew the answer to that. He'd been miserable. And yet it felt so tempting to just go back to that world. Maybe it was easier working for corporate clients he cared nothing about than staring into the eyes of a vulnerable man.

David stepped into Caroline's, a popular dining spot. The restaurant was nearly empty—it was almost closing time. Finding a table near the back, David ordered a slice of blueberry cobbler, Benny's favorite dessert, from the friendly waitress. The booth was the exact same spot where David had had his first real conversation with the old man last year. Staring at the empty seat across the table from him, David could still see Benny sitting there in his black trench coat, smiling ear to ear, while they talked about life and munched on two pieces of delicious blueberry cobbler. It seemed like yesterday.

"My name's David."

"Like the shepherd," Benny replied.

David tilted his head. "Sorry?"

Benny smiled again, pointed at the small Bible sitting on the table. "From the Scriptures. David was a shepherd. First, with the animals. Eventually, he was a shepherd to God's people. You have a distinguished name, my friend."

David shrugged. "I guess. But I'm no shepherd."

"Not yet, maybe."

David's reflective moment got interrupted by the voice of a man who was suddenly standing near him. "Most lawyers I know head to the bars for a drink after work. You come here to get dessert?"

David looked up and noticed Keith Carter, the fiftysomething man with the crew cut who worked with the Texas Veterans Legal Assistance Project.

"I'm too broke to drink right now," David replied.

"I hate to hear that."

"You following me around or something?" David asked. "Are you that desperate to find poor veterans to help?"

Carter smiled, adjusted his square-framed brown glasses. "Nah, just spotted you while passing by outside. Mind if I sit?"

David shrugged, held out a palm. "Suit yourself."

Carter sat opposite David. The waitress immediately came over to take his order. "I'll have what he's having," Carter told her, nodding at the cobbler.

"Best in town," David said. "Trust me."

"I'll be the judge of that." Carter put his elbows up on the table. "You look like you've had a rough day. Things not going well on the Roger North case?"

"Let's just say I got thrown a major curveball today."

"Curveballs were *always* my nemesis. Could never hit them."

"You played baseball?"

"Yep, a lifetime ago. Spent two years in Double-A ball with the Richmond Flying Squirrels. I could crush a fastball but could never hit the damn bender. What about you? You play any ball?"

"Football. Until my knee gave out."

The waitress quickly returned with another slice of cobbler. Carter took a big bite and made a humming noise like he really enjoyed it.

"Can't argue with you," Carter admitted. "This is really good."

David finished off his piece, put the fork down, sat all the way back in the booth, feeling satisfied. "So how long you been with this veterans' organization?"

"About five years, give or take. I was an English professor at the University of Houston for twenty years. I got a call one day from a guy I served with way back who was down on his luck and needed some help with a precarious legal situation. I stepped in and helped walk my friend through a complicated legal matter. I liked the feeling of helping an old vet like myself so much that I left my teaching gig and got a job with VLAP. So here I am."

"Badgering strangers?"

"Strangers? We're sharing dessert together. Are we not friends yet?"

They exchanged a quick grin. David liked Carter's easygoing way.

"So how long you been a lawyer?" Carter asked.

"About a year."

"And you're already handling a murder case? How does that happen?"

"Dumb luck, I think."

"Did you know Roger North before becoming his lawyer?"

"Nope. Just met him."

"So why take the case?"

"I blame the ghost of a street preacher."

"The ghost of *who*?"

"It's a long story."

"I have all night. I love ghost stories."

"I don't, sorry. I'm tired. Maybe another day."

David stood to leave, but Carter stopped him.

"Hey, you think I could talk to him, David?"

"Who? My client?"

"Yeah. Maybe I could stabilize the situation for you. You know, vet to vet. We tend to speak a different code than other people. It might calm him down and be a help to you."

"What makes you think he needs to be calmed down?"

Carter shrugged. "I heard he tried to choke his lawyer an hour ago."

David gave him a quizzical smile. "Just walking by, huh?"

"We just want to help, David. I think you could use it."

Unfortunately, David needed more help than Carter could give him.

"Have a good night," he said.

TWENTY-FOUR

David returned to his office around eleven that night. Standing outside the main door to the suite, he could hear the mutt yapping away in the back room. He'd put the dog back there with a bowl of food and water. There was no telling what all Sandy had destroyed over the last few hours. Pulling his key out, David noticed the front door to their office suite was unlocked, which was unusual. He was certain he'd locked up everything before leaving earlier that night. Maybe Doc was waiting for him inside? When he opened the door, David found that all the office lights were off. Then he heard a clanking noise come from somewhere in the darkness of the suite—it wasn't from the dog in the back room.

"Doc?" David called out. "You in here?"

No response. No other sounds. Maybe he was hearing things. Stepping fully into the front entry room, David reached for the light switch on the wall. Before getting there, he heard shoes shuffle on the hardwood floor behind him. David turned, searched. A figure suddenly appeared from the dark and tackled him hard to the floor. David felt the air go right out of his lungs. What the hell? The strong figure was directly on top of him. Struggling, David reached up, stuck his hand in a bearded face. Then a swift punch hit David's left cheek, knocking his head sideways, sending a jolt through him. David swung wildly in return with his right fist, hitting the intruder in the rib section. The man grunted in pain, rocked back, and David took that opportunity to shove him off.

Picking himself up off the floor, David rushed toward the man, driving him into the table, sending both of them flipping over it and then splattering onto the floor again on the other side. Another hard punch found David's left ear, making him dizzy for a second. A second punch grazed his jawline. Feeling around on the floor beside him, David's fingers came across a bottle—probably the empty bottle of Guinness he'd left on the table earlier that night. Clutching it, he swung and smashed the bottle against the man's head, shattering it and sending glass flying. The man let out a yell, fell backward. David tried to push himself up, but his hand landed square on a shard of broken glass on the floor, puncturing the skin, and he dropped again in pain.

Instead of another attack, the intruder tried to escape out the front door. David lunged after him, grabbing the man by one of his combat boots, trying to stop him. But that only got him a quick kick to the stomach from the man's opposite boot, which left David curled up and gasping for air. The man bolted out the door into the hallway. Picking himself up, David staggered forward into the hallway. He could hear the intruder bounding down the stairwell around the corner. David chased as best he could, descending three steps at a time, and pursued the figure out of the building. When he hit the main sidewalk, David whipped his head back and forth in both directions.

The man was gone.

TWENTY-FIVE

Pounding on the main office door woke David from sleep. It wasn't so much the steady knocking out front as it was the dog now growling on the sofa at his feet. David reached down, snagged his phone from the floor. Six forty-five? Who was out there this early? He tried to shake off the fuzziness of his mind, which was probably more a result of the punches to his head last night than the early hour. Although he'd taken a handful of Tylenol, his head was still throbbing. Had he walked into the middle of a robbery? Had one of his street clients gotten that desperate? Or was it something else? His gut said it was something else. Although his personal office was a bit ransacked, David couldn't find a single valuable missing. He'd thought of calling the police but decided against it. What would be the point? He couldn't identify the guy in any significant way.

More knocking out front. Whoever was out there had to know David had been sleeping at the office, or they wouldn't go to so much trouble. Probably one of his street friends, hoping Lori had put something new to eat in the mini fridge. A couple of the guys seemed to watch their office night and day in anticipation of Thomas's wife showing up with a fresh batch of homemade goodness. David couldn't really blame them—Lori was one hell of a cook.

Cursing, David swung his bare feet to the floor. He looked down at his right hand, which was wrapped in white bandages. Although the cut from the glass shard hurt like hell, he didn't think he needed any serious medical attention. He certainly didn't want to spend money on an emergency room visit right now. He grabbed his jeans, pulled them on, and then stumbled down the hallway to the front room, the dog following at his heels.

More steady knocking, which was really annoying him.

"Hold on!" David yelled, unlocking the door.

He swung it wide-open, ready to berate whoever thought it was a good idea to come by the office at this ridiculous hour. However, his anger was quickly replaced by shock. Neil Mason was standing in the hallway, wearing his usual high-dollar suit, hair done perfectly, as if he'd already been at the office for several hours.

"Morning, sunshine," Mason said with a snarky grin.

"What the hell are you doing here?"

"Waking you up, clearly. We need to talk."

"You couldn't call first?"

"We need to talk in person, David. Can I come inside?"

"Yeah, sure, whatever."

Opening the door, David allowed Mason into the entry room, offered him a chair at the round table. The dog began investigating the man's ankles. David wouldn't mind if Sandy raised a leg on Mason's shoes.

"They let you keep a dog in here?" Mason asked him.

"Belongs to a friend. You want some coffee?"

"Sure."

Walking to the back room, David stepped up to the coffee maker on the foldout table and found the glass carafe still half-full from the previous day. It would do. He poured the remains of the container into two small mugs, stuck them both in the microwave for a few seconds, and then returned to Mason.

"I like what you've done with the place," Mason deadpanned, looking around. "This office double as a pawnshop?"

"Yes, I'll give you fifty bucks for that obnoxious gold watch."

"This watch was a gift from Senator Lorenzo."

"Then make it twenty bucks."

David handed Mason a mug, took a seat across from him.

Mason took a sip, nearly spit it out. "You trying to poison me?"

"Guess you'll find out in about sixty seconds."

David took a big gulp, as if it didn't bother him.

"What happened to your hand?" Mason asked, noticing the bandages.

"Fishing accident," David lied. "What do you want, Neil?"

Setting his mug down, Mason leaned forward. "I want to talk about the case."

"Yeah, I didn't figure you showed up here to offer decorating advice."

"You can be a real ass at seven in the morning."

"You can be a real ass every hour of the day."

Mason grinned. "Touché."

"What about the case?" David asked. "You finally dropping all charges?"

"No, but I am here to offer you a deal."

This time David didn't have a smart-ass reply. He was too stunned. "What kind of deal?"

"Twenty years. He could be out in ten."

It took all the willpower David could muster to keep his jaw from dropping onto the table. Twenty years, out in ten? That was a far cry from going after the death penalty. Considering the mounting evidence David kept finding against his own client, the unexpected plea offer felt like a gift from the legal gods. He should be jumping for joy right now. But something didn't feel right.

"Why the sudden change of heart?" David managed to ask. "Two days ago, it was nothing but 'death penalty this, death penalty that.'"

"Believe me, this is not my idea," Mason admitted. "I'd love nothing more than to go to trial and completely humiliate you. But Jordan wants to spare Murphy's widow the agony of a trial. This has already been painful enough for Michelle and the kids. He doesn't want them to have to relive it all in vivid detail in a few months just to put a complete mental case like your client on a long road toward his eventual death. Reluctantly, I agree with him. Let's give Michelle some immediate closure, so she can begin healing right away."

"That's kindhearted of you both."

It was also total BS. David knew that Jordan couldn't care less about sparing Michelle from a trial. Not with the coming election. What was really going on?

"Don't act so shocked," Mason continued. "In spite of what you may think, I'm not a bad guy. Believe it or not, David, I think we could be friends. In a lot of ways, you remind me of . . . well, me."

"Great, let's go tandem biking."

Mason frowned, as if already tiring of having to put on this friendly act. He put out a hand. "Do we have a deal or what?"

David didn't shake it. "I'll have to consult with my client first, of course."

"Of course." Mason dropped his hand, didn't look at all happy with that initial response. "I'll give you until the end of the day. Then all bets are off."

TWENTY-SIX

This time, the jail deputy left the handcuffs on Rebel. David didn't argue with him. Not after his client had tried to choke him last night. They sat across from each other in the private room. Rebel seemed to have calmed down. He even looked remorseful sitting there, staring at his cuffed hands with droopy eyes.

"Real sorry about last night," Rebel offered. "You still my lawyer?"

"Yes."

"I just hate being called crazy, that's all. No excuses, though."

"No, it's my fault. I shouldn't have provoked you." David stuck out his bandaged right hand. "Friends again?"

"Yes, sir." Rebel shook it. "What happened to your hand?"

"Got into a fight with a guy last night."

Rebel grinned. "Two peas in a pod, you and me. Hope he got the worst of it."

"I've got some news, Rebel. The DA is offering a deal."

"Really? They ain't hell-bent on sticking the needle in me anymore?"

"Apparently not. They're offering twenty years. You could be out in ten."

Rebel took in that news but didn't respond right away.

"What do you think?" David finally asked.

Rebel seemed contemplative. "I think I might have met that man at one of the free breakfasts the Methodist church puts on for the homeless each week."

"Who? Luke Murphy?"

Rebel nodded. "He was volunteering."

"Did you talk to him?"

Another nod. More reflective thought.

"What did y'all talk about?" David asked.

"Don't remember. But he was real nice and friendly."

"You think that's why you had his business card in your backpack?"

"Maybe. I don't know." His eyes met David's. "You think I could have killed a man without even remembering it?"

David could tell it was a sincere question. "I think we're all capable of doing really bad things when we're not operating in our right minds."

"My mind hasn't been right for a long time, Lawyer."

"I found the Clozaril prescription in your backpack. Does it help you?"

Rebel shrugged. "A little."

"But you haven't been taking it?"

He shook his head. "Nah, makes me numb all over. I hate it."

"I could get a doctor in here. Try different medications. See if we could find one that works better for you."

"I hate doctors more than lawyers."

David didn't push. It was not the most important thing today.

"What do you think I should do, Lawyer? Take the deal?"

"I think the DA has a good case against us."

"So we'd lose?"

"If we went to trial, I'd certainly do everything I could."

"But we'd still lose?"

"Today, yes." David thought about the mystery woman. "But a lot can still happen between now and a trial."

"I see." He leaned back in his chair. "How come you've never asked me for any money? Ain't no such thing as a free lawyer in this country. A case like this would probably cost me ten thousand dollars with one of those big law firms."

"Probably twenty times that, actually."

"You serious?"

David nodded. He thought about the money he'd found in Rebel's backpack. "Moses said you always seem to have cash on you. Why's that?"

Rebel shrugged. "My uncle left me a little something when he passed. I get by here and there with it. But you ain't asking me to pay you a dime. How come?"

"I'm happy to take whatever you can manage, believe me. But I have other reasons for doing this."

Rebel's eyes narrowed. "Benny meant a lot to you, didn't he?"

"Yes, he did."

"You know, Benny took me down to the river one day, and he baptized me in the name of the Father, the Son, and the Holy Spirit. Told me I never had to be afraid of death again."

"Are you afraid?"

Rebel shrugged. "Hadn't really thought too much about it until now."

"Well, the clock is ticking. We have until midnight to accept."

"What if I'm innocent?"

"In the court of law, the only thing that matters is what we can prove."

"Ten years is a long time for a man like me to be locked up."

"Take the day to think about it."

TWENTY-SEVEN

Luke Murphy's funeral service was held at the Methodist church downtown. Several hundred people were in attendance. David sat near the back and damn near cried his eyes out when Michelle walked down the middle aisle to the very front with her two small kids at her side. Regardless of the DA's motives, David knew that Mason was probably right. Accepting the plea deal and avoiding the trial would likely be the best thing for Michelle and the family. But David still couldn't comprehend the sudden change of course—especially with everything he'd found out through his own investigation.

David scanned the crowd. It looked like the entire DA's office was in attendance. Jeff Jordan and Neil Mason sat near the front of the sanctuary. Dana Mitchem sat with other colleagues two rows behind them. A minister started the service with a prayer. A choir sang hymns. Then two of Murphy's high school friends offered some words and stories about Murphy, getting a few laughs here and there. Under other circumstances, David thought he might have been asked to say something. But he understood why he had not. Still, it stung. Murphy was a good friend. Had he made the right choice? After the minister led the service, the choir sang a closing song. Then everyone was invited to a reception in the fellowship hall next door. Michelle and the family exited first, and the rest of the crowd was dismissed.

David hung around the back, waiting for Dana. After talking with her colleagues, she finally came over to where he stood alone in the back corner of the room.

The hug between them was extra tight.

"This was nice," David offered.

"Murphy would have hated it," Dana countered. "He didn't like being the center of attention."

"That's true. Remember when I gave him that fake award at our team party after nationals? Wow, the look on his face."

"I thought he was going to punch you."

"Believe me, he took it out on me on the basketball court the next day. I think I still have the bruises to prove it."

They shared a brief smile.

"I'm really going to miss him, Dana."

"Me, too. He was like a big brother."

Another quiet moment before Dana broke the silence.

"I heard about the plea offer this morning," she said.

"Doesn't make sense. Why'd Mason do it?"

"I don't know. He didn't consult with me."

"You have to know *something*."

"We're all a bit shocked by it," Dana admitted. "Yesterday, everything was full steam ahead. And then it all changed overnight for some reason."

"Did you show Mason the video of the girl I sent you?"

She nodded. "And I told him about Murphy possibly being at the bar with her just minutes before his death."

"What did he say?"

"He was dismissive of the whole thing. But I could tell it caught his interest. Then I saw Jordan in Mason's office late last night. I didn't catch too much, but they were definitely talking about Murphy's case.

124

I heard Jordan mention pressure to close things off and make it all go away. *Nice and tidy* were his exact words."

"Pressure? From where?"

She shook her head. "No idea."

"Did you find anything in Murphy's files or work contacts connecting him to the initials *KP*?"

"Nothing. And I promise you, I checked thoroughly."

David sighed. "None of this feels right, Dana."

"Just take the deal."

TWENTY-EIGHT

David huddled with Thomas back at the office. They spent an hour diagramming every possible angle of Rebel's case on a portable whiteboard. The board was now covered with notes, circles, and arrows that connected everything together. David stared at the board and shook his head. The DA had an overwhelming case against his client. So it made zero sense that they were now offering him a deal.

And not just any deal—a generous deal.

"I think we take the deal," Thomas said.

"What if Rebel doesn't want to take it?"

"You're a good lawyer. You lead him to that smart conclusion."

Sitting at his desk, David ran his fingers through his hair. The mutt was curled up in his lap. He had to admit he was kind of enjoying having the dog around. "We're missing something, Thomas. Why does Jordan suddenly want this case to just go away? Look at the board, man. It doesn't make *any* sense."

"It doesn't have to make sense. Let's just accept the gift and move on. This was our aim when we initially took the case. Get Rebel a deal. Well, mission accomplished."

"But we're onto something, and for whatever reason, they don't want us to continue to pursue it."

"We can't play games with a man's life, David."

"I know, I know." David turned, stared out over Congress Avenue. "Dana said she suspects someone is putting pressure on Jordan."

"So what? The man works in politics. I'm sure he gets pressured from everywhere all the time. Get your client on board, and put this whole thing to bed. Besides, we could use the extra time right now to start packing up the office."

David groaned at that comment, which made the dog perk up. Thomas then left him alone with the cluttered board.

"What do you think, Sandy? Should we take the deal?"

The mutt just bobbed his head at him curiously.

A new text notification arrived on his phone. He picked up the phone off his desk, stared at the screen. No name, just an anonymous local number. However, he noticed it was the same random person who had texted him the news article link yesterday about the young man who was recently killed outside the Tejano nightclub.

Mr. Adams, if you receive this in the next few minutes, please respond. More details to follow. It's about the Luke Murphy case.

His eyes narrowed. The text was grammatically correct. That wasn't usually the case with the random texts he often received from the streets. He sometimes had to pull out his decoder ring to decipher those illiterate messages.

He typed a reply.

I'm here.

A second text arrived seconds later.

JW Marriott bar. Two men are sitting at the end of the bar. One is wearing a blue suit with a yellow tie. You should check them out.

David typed:

Why?

He waited, but there was no immediate response. He typed again.

Hello? Who are these men? Who are you?

More waiting. Still no response. He did a quick Google search for the random phone number and found nothing that connected it to any specific person or business.

Who was it?

David read the message again. JW Marriott?

Sighing, David set the dog down, headed for the door.

TWENTY-NINE

The JW Marriott was a short two-block walk south on Congress from his office building. David couldn't be sure if this was legit—still, he hustled. He entered the glass doors of the opulent hotel lobby, peered over to his right. The spacious bar lounge was connected to the wide-open lobby with dozens of comfortable seating arrangements. The bar was packed with people on this late afternoon, a likely mix of hotel guests and the downtown business crowd. David circled around the outside of the lounge and slipped onto a stool at the end of the main bar.

Peering ten stools down from him, David spotted a man probably in his thirties wearing a blue suit and yellow tie. He was the only guy in a blue suit and yellow tie that David currently saw sitting at the bar. He didn't recognize him. The guy had brown hair combed perfectly to the side and looked like a preppy banker. He was talking to another man of similar age who wore a gray suit. The second man had a goatee, wore glasses, and was prematurely balding on top. He looked like David's grade school science teacher. David didn't recognize the second guy, either. Who were they?

David ordered a beer when the bartender came over to him. While pretending to be on his phone, he raised it up just enough to take a pic of the banker and the teacher. He quickly texted the photo to the random number.

Okay, I'm here. Now what?

He stared at his screen, but no reply came back to him. He was beginning to lose his patience. Still, he watched both men. Their discussion did not seem light of heart. There were no smiles, laughs, or easy banter between them. Both men looked quite pensive. Lots of frowning and squinting. Ten minutes after David had arrived, the meeting between the two men appeared to be over. Both men stood up from their stools and headed for the hotel lobby doors.

Setting cash down for his drink, David slipped off his stool and quickly walked over to where the two men had just been sitting. He glanced at the signed credit card receipt still sitting on top of the bar. The banker had a somewhat legible signature. David pulled out his phone, made sure no one was watching, and casually snapped a photo of the receipt before the bartender came back over to grab it.

Then David hurried through the bar and out the glass doors of the hotel. He peered in both directions. The sidewalk in front of the hotel was packed with late-afternoon travelers. He put himself in the middle of the crowd, searching faces coming toward him and the backs of those headed in the opposite direction.

But couldn't spot either guy. They were already gone.

THIRTY

The clock was ticking on Mason's deadline for accepting the plea deal. David had only a half hour left to make the call. Mason had already texted him multiple times, demanding to know his answer. David kept pushing him off. It was time to go see Rebel, who was probably a nervous wreck right now, wondering if his lawyer was going to show up before midnight. David still wasn't sure in what direction to lead Rebel. This afternoon's text messages and his monitoring of a hotel bar meeting between the two men had only muddied the waters for him. The anonymous texter had implied the bar meeting was about Murphy's case. How? And why had this same person texted him the article yesterday about the guy who was killed in a drug deal? What the hell was going on? He'd sent several texts back to the original phone number but still hadn't received a response. Whoever was on the other end wasn't communicating with him at this point. Why?

Sitting at his desk, David stared at his laptop screen. He'd run Google searches on several variations of the signature on the bar receipt before finally finding the guy. The banker was actually a real estate attorney named Lee Barksdale who worked for a big firm called Sewell & Merritt. Barksdale's website profile page had his smiling photo and said he'd earned his undergrad degree at LSU, went to law school at Dartmouth, and had been practicing law with Sewell & Merritt for the past eight years. None of this information meant much to David. An online search trying to connect Barksdale to Murphy turned up nothing. At least there didn't appear to be any formal connection between the two men.

David couldn't stall any longer. Grabbing his jacket, he left the office and made the quick walk over to the criminal justice complex, where he found himself sitting in the private jail room a few minutes later. Although the room was frigid as usual, David could feel sweat beading up under his armpits. A deputy led Rebel inside and took off the handcuffs, per David's request.

"Where you been, Lawyer?" Rebel asked, sitting.

"Sorry. I was trying to sort some things out." He showed Rebel the photo on his phone of the two men from the bar. "You recognize either of these guys?"

Rebel stared down at the screen, his face bunched. "Nope."

"Take a second look. This could be important."

After more squinting at the phone, Rebel shook his head. "Ain't never seen them. Who are they?"

"They may or may not have something to do with your case." David then showed him the news article about the guy who was killed outside the nightclub. "This mean anything to you?"

"Nope. What's this all about?"

"I haven't figured it out just yet. You still can't remember *anything* else about that night in the alley?"

"I keep trying. But ain't nothing more coming to me."

"What about what Moses said about you going to *settle a score?*"

"Hell, that could be anyone. I got so many people trying to screw me over."

David sighed, ran his fingers through his hair. He felt the heavy weight of the moment. He was out of options and time.

"So what're we going to do, Lawyer?" Rebel asked.

David looked up, swallowed. "I think we accept the deal."

Although saying the words felt like a punch to the gut, David knew Thomas was right—he couldn't play around with a man's life.

Rebel gave him a half grin. "You just saying that because you're scared?"

"Damn right, I am," David admitted. "This is not a game. This is your life."

Rebel actually laughed, taking David off guard.

"You find this funny?" David asked.

"Nah, I don't. But you know that question you asked me earlier today? Was I afraid of death? Well, I done thought about it all day, and guess what? I ain't afraid. I really do believe what Benny always said. *Therefore, there is now no condemnation for those who are in Christ Jesus, because through Christ Jesus the law of the Spirit who gives life has set you free from the law of sin and death.* You ever read that before, Lawyer?"

"Probably. Mom had me in church every Sunday."

"Romans Eight," Rebel clarified. "Words of freedom."

David cocked his head. "So what are you saying, Rebel? Are you telling me you actually want to go to trial? Despite my advisement against it?"

"Damn right. I ain't afraid. You shouldn't be afraid, either."

David had to admit, he was glad to hear Rebel say that. But he had to make sure his client was coming to this decision all by himself. "I turn this deal down, we can't go back. You understand that?"

"Either way, the truth will set me free."

Minutes later, David stood on a quiet sidewalk outside the county jail. The time on his phone said eleven fifty-seven. Three minutes to the deadline. With shaky fingers, he typed out a brief text message to Mason, stared at it for a few seconds in disbelief. Taking a deep breath, he pressed "Send."

No deal. See you in court.

THIRTY-ONE

Sleep was near impossible. Mason had immediately responded to David's late-night text message turning down the plea deal with a string of angry expletives and basically called him the stupidest and most reckless attorney who'd probably ever walked the earth. Staring at the ceiling in the back room all night, David wondered if that was true. Giving up on sleep around four in the morning, he sat at his office desk and researched the news article sent to him by the anonymous phone number. The twenty-three-year-old man who was killed in the nightclub parking lot a week ago was named Eduardo Martinez from Del Valle, a lower-income community on the fringe of East Austin. According to the article, Martinez had been employed by the City of Austin for the past two years as part of a facility maintenance crew. Martinez's 2001 Mazda hatchback was found at the scene of the crime with small amounts of heroin inside. Police suspected a drug deal. No suspects had been arrested. David read several other similar online articles that basically summarized the same information.

Who was Eduardo Martinez?

Why had this mystery person texted him the article?

David stared at an online photo of Eduardo Martinez, which looked like it had been taken from his city ID. The guy had dark hair combed neatly to the side, was clean-shaven and smiling. A small tear-drop tattoo sat below his left eye. He didn't necessarily look like a drug dealer. Using an online background check, David found a misdemeanor DUI charge from four years ago but nothing else.

When the sun finally popped up outside his office window, David jumped in his truck and drove through East Austin, out past the airport, until he reached the Del Valle community. Using the address from the criminal background check, he located a small redbrick home on a street lined with nearly matching homes. A gray minivan was parked in the driveway. David noticed a couple of tricycles and scooters in the tiny but well-maintained front yard. The neighborhood was just starting to wake, as cars and trucks began pulling out of various driveways.

David parked on the curb outside the home. From a property search, David knew the house belonged to Hector and Sayra Martinez, whom he guessed were Eduardo Martinez's parents. Getting out of his truck, David followed the short driveway to a brown front door and knocked. Seconds later, a heavyset woman in her fifties answered the door.

"Ms. Martinez?" David asked.

"Yes, can I help you?"

"I hope so. My name's David Adams. I'm a local attorney. Sorry to intrude on you first thing this morning, ma'am, but I wondered if I could have a few minutes to speak with you about Eduardo?"

Hearing his name immediately made her eyes water.

"We had his funeral just yesterday," she stated.

"Was he your son?"

She nodded. "Why do you want to talk to me about Eddie?"

"My deepest condolences, Ms. Martinez. I wouldn't even bother you today if it wasn't really important." David noticed two small children running around in the interior of the house. "I think there's a possibility his death could somehow be connected to another legal matter with a client I'm representing."

"My son was a good boy," she said, eyes narrowing. "What the TV and papers have all said about him is not true. Eddie was no drug dealer. If there were drugs in his car, they weren't his, I can promise you that, Mr. Adams. Eddie had two kids here to feed and a good job, so he would never go near that trash. He's been so responsible and helpful to me, especially since my husband died last year."

"I understand. Do you know who he might have been meeting with in the parking lot of that bar the other night?"

She shook her head. "I don't know. Eddie and his friends went to that bar all the time. He liked to have a good time, but he wasn't a troublemaker. I told the police the same thing. I don't think they believed me or cared much. So I don't believe they're even out there looking for who shot him. But I wish they would go looking for my daughter right now."

She covered her mouth with a trembling hand, a new tear falling onto her chubby cheek.

"Your daughter?"

"I haven't heard from my Mia for the past four days. I'm worried sick. I know something is wrong."

"Does she live with you?"

"No, Mia is a law student at UT. She lives near campus. She texted me a couple of days after her brother's death, said she was going to take off for a week or two, but I was not to worry. That was the last I've heard from her."

"But you are worried?"

Her brow raised and pulled together. "Mia didn't show up at Eddie's service yesterday. She would've *never* missed her brother's funeral unless something bad had happened to her. Mia and Eddie were like best friends."

"Did you call the police?"

"Yes, of course, but they said there was nothing they could do, especially with what Mia had texted me. Mia is an adult. The police said they had no reason to try to find her. Can *you* help me, Mr. Adams?"

David wondered if Mia could possibly be the same woman from the security video. Although the *KP* initials didn't match up, could she be the woman who'd met with Murphy at the Dirty Dog and who had approached him outside the county jail the other night?

"I'll try. Do you have a photo?"

"Of course."

Letting him inside the foyer, Ms. Martinez handed him a framed photo of her daughter. David studied it carefully. She was not the same woman from the security video. Although Mia had medium-length black hair and a thin build, she had brown eyes—not green eyes. Still, she might be involved somehow.

"Can you give me her address?" David asked.

Ms. Martinez wrote down her daughter's address on a piece of paper. Holding out his cell phone, David showed her photos of Murphy, along with the two men from the hotel bar yesterday.

"Do you recognize any of these men, Ms. Martinez?"

She examined them closely. "Isn't this the man who was just murdered downtown? It's been all over the news lately."

"Yes. Any chance Eddie knew him?"

"He never said anything to me."

"What about the other two men?"

"I'm sorry, Mr. Adams. I've never seen them before."

THIRTY-TWO

David parked in front of a yellowed old building four blocks north of UT's campus and located the front door of Mia's unit on the second floor. He knocked twice and waited. There was no answer and no sound of movement on the other side of the door. He tried to peek into the square window by the door, but the blinds were sealed tight. He knocked again, but still no response. Then he looked down at the doorknob and noticed there was a small chunk of wood missing from around the lock mechanism. Staring closer at the latch, he thought it looked like someone had jimmied it with a tool. Had someone broken into the apartment? Reaching down, David turned the doorknob, felt a chill push through him. The door was unlocked.

Cracking the door open, he called out, "Hello? Mia? Anyone here?"

No response. He pushed the door farther open, then cursed. He could immediately tell the apartment had been ransacked. Directly in front of him was a living room with a sofa and a chair, the cushions of which were flung about, a coffee table in the middle flipped completely upside down. A small desk that sat against the wall had all the drawers pulled out. The drawers were lying on the worn carpet, with papers, pens, folders, books, binders scattered beneath them. The kitchen to the right looked the same as the living space. Half the cabinet drawers were pulled wide-open, most of their contents on the kitchen floor.

David nearly jumped out of his skin when he heard a noise coming from down the short hallway to the bedroom. Was someone still inside? He grabbed the closest weapon he could find—a frying pan—and took a few steps into the hallway. Another rustling noise sent a jolt through him. The light was on in the only bathroom. He took a quick peek inside. No one was there. The bedroom was next. The door was cracked open, and the light was off.

He thought about Mia, his throat thick. Was he about to find her? Had something bad already happened to her? His grip tightened on the pan in his right fist, and he pushed the bedroom door farther open. The bedroom was also in complete disarray. Boxes were tossed around, with books and binders spread out all over the bed and the carpet. The noise again. From the other side of the disheveled bed. David stepped over boxes, held his breath, and glanced around the bed. A brown cat bounced up and bolted straight for the door, scaring the hell out of him.

David quickly backtracked to the front of the apartment. He took another quick scan of the room. Who had been here? And what were they looking for? He wondered if he should call the police; however, he decided against it. Not until he had a chance to explore Mia's disappearance. Getting the police involved at this point could complicate and perhaps compromise his own investigation.

Stepping outside onto the walkway, he pulled the front door closed behind him. A neighbor two doors down exited her apartment at that same moment and looked over at him. She was probably around the same age as Mia—midtwenties—with a blonde ponytail, jeans, and a UT Law School T-shirt.

"Have you seen Mia?" David asked.

"Not in a few days," she replied. "Who are you?"

"A friend of her mom's. She asked me to stop by and check on her."

"Mia's probably over at the law school library. She's hardly ever home. She studies every second of the day. I wish I had her kind of discipline."

THIRTY-THREE

David entered the main building of UT's law school, which sat on the northeast corner of the sprawling university campus. He immediately recognized the familiar academic sounds and smells, as well as the exhaustion etched into the faces of the students who crossed back in forth in front of him. Two years ago, he'd been one of them, fighting his guts out to finish as high in his class as possible, eager to get recruited by the best law firms in the country.

He found his way over to the Tarlton Law Library, began searching for the brunette who liked to wear a burnt-orange UT baseball cap nearly everywhere—according to the many photos he'd found of Mia on Facebook. David moved in and out of the library rows and around the study tables. When he didn't spot Mia anywhere, he began asking around and flashing her photo to other students, while telling them he was recruiting for one of the local firms.

Several students said they had classes with Mia, but she hadn't attended them all week. A couple of them knew she'd had a death in the family and figured she'd temporarily stepped away from school to deal with it. David was about to give up altogether when he talked to a girl named Alicia in a student lounge who seemed to be closer to Mia than some of her other classmates.

"Sure, I'm friends with Mia," Alicia said. "Is she okay?"

"I don't know. That's why I'm trying to find her."

"Did you check with her mom?"

"I just came from her mom's house. She's *really* worried."

"Oh, okay. Mia's brother's death really rocked her hard."

"I would imagine so," David replied.

"No, it was more than just grief. She really wigged out about it."

"What do you mean?"

"I met up with Mia four days ago. She gave me one of her class papers and asked me to turn it in to Professor Albert. Mia told me she had to check out for a bit and didn't know when she'd be back. But she wasn't a sobbing mess, which surprised me. Honestly, it was more like she was scared."

"Scared of what?"

Alicia shrugged. "I asked. She didn't want to talk about it."

"Any idea where she might go to *check out?*"

Alicia tugged a strand of curly red hair. "Not really. I figured she went to stay with her mom, but I guess not. She's been dating this guy in a band. I think his name is Scott, but I can't be too sure."

"Do you know the name of the band?"

"Something weird . . . maybe the Dragon Puppets? I think they play funky heavy-metal stuff—which is not really my thing."

"I really appreciate your help."

"Sure. I hope she's okay. I've texted her several times this week but haven't heard anything back." Alicia's nose wrinkled. "Hey, aren't you the attorney in that prosecutor's murder case that's been all over the news?"

"Yes, I am."

"Is that why you're looking for Mia?"

David cocked his head. "Why would you ask that?"

"I don't know. It's just that I saw Mia meeting with that guy in the courtyard here the same day he was killed."

"Luke Murphy?"

"Yes. I didn't know who he was at the time. But I figured it out *after* the news broke of his death. I never got the chance to ask Mia about it, though."

THIRTY-FOUR

David received an urgent phone call later that morning from Larue, his young friend with the cornrows and baggy jeans, saying he had a person David needed to see ASAP. He met up with Larue on the sidewalk right outside Pete's Dueling Piano Bar. The bars along Sixth Street were all closed this morning, so the sidewalks were nearly empty.

Larue introduced the young guy standing with him as Skater. The teenager was thin, with orange spiky hair, and his skinny arms were covered with tattoos—most of which looked like scenes from *Star Wars* movies. Although he hadn't met Skater before, David thought he remembered seeing him holding a cardboard sign near his office building, where he was begging for money and food. The kid didn't look strung out, which was sadly how David found most of the street kids who camped on the downtown sidewalks.

"Good to meet you," David said.

"Yes, sir. You, too."

"Tell him what you told me, Skater," Larue urged the kid.

"All right. See, I was hanging out over by the convention center this morning, like I usually do, just minding my own business, you know, when this dude suddenly comes up to me and starts talking. He asks me how long I been on the streets and if I do drugs and all that. I ain't perfect, mister, but I told him I'm no druggie. I figured he may have been a doctor or something, maybe from one of them charity deals, 'cause he wanted to check me out and shined a tiny flashlight in my eyes and stuff. I guess to see if I was lying and was high on drugs. He gave me a bag of food from Whataburger, so I didn't really care much."

"Get to the other part already," Larue suggested.

"Yeah, so, we was just talking a bit, see, and then the guy asks me if I'd be interested in making a thousand dollars. I thought he was wanting a trick or something, so I was like, nah, dude, I don't do that. But he said it wasn't anything like that. He asked me if I'd heard about the guy who was murdered by the homeless dude in the alley over here. I was, like, yeah, man, I done heard. Everyone knows about it. Then he says he'll give me a thousand cash if I'll go to the police, tell them I was in the alley where it all happened the other night, and that I saw that homeless guy straight up shoot the man."

David felt a shot of adrenaline race up his spine. "What did you tell him?"

"I said I didn't want no trouble with the police. But he said I wouldn't get in any trouble. He'd give me everything I'd need. A photo of the shooter, a description. I just had to stick with the script, and I'd get paid. Then he pulled five hundred bucks out of his pocket, said I could have it right there. And I would get the rest of the cash when I followed through with everything."

"Tell him what happened next, bro," Larue said, clearly eager to get to it.

"I turned the dude down again. See, I have a warrant out for me for petty theft back in El Paso, so I ain't looking to mess around with no police. I don't even want them to know about me being here. This guy gets real pissed, pulls out a gun, and sticks it right in my face. He says to me if I tell *anyone* about our conversation, he'll come find me again and put a bullet in my skull. I swear I won't say nothing, so he finally leaves me alone."

"What did the guy look like, Skater?" David asked.

Skater shrugged his frail shoulders. "Probably about your age, I dunno, but around the same height as you. He was bald, though, with kind of a scruffy beard."

"What was he wearing?"

"Like a black jacket, I think, and, like, black combat boots."

Combat boots? David thought about the man who'd attacked him inside his office the other night. He'd had a beard and wore combat boots. "Anything else?"

Skater pointed to side of his head right above the eyebrow. "Yeah, the dude had a white bandage on his head right about here above his eye."

David cursed. The same place where he'd swung the beer bottle to get the guy off him. Who was he? "Why did you come tell Larue after this guy threatened you with a gun to keep your mouth shut?"

Skater shrugged again. "Larue's my boy, see? Simple as that. Larue's been good to me ever since I got to town a few months back. Always making sure I find something to eat and stay in the right places. Larue has been asking around for help on this deal with the Rebel dude, so I came and told him."

"You did real good, Skater," Larue commended him. "We got to look out for each other."

"I appreciate this info," David agreed. "Will you let Larue know if you see this guy around again?"

"Sure, man. I ain't going to forget that face anytime soon."

THIRTY-FIVE

Back in his office, David researched local bands and tried to find a heavy-metal group who called themselves Dragon Puppets. He had no luck with *puppets* but did find a band called Dragon *Parrots*. A crappy website showed them to be three young guys with long grungy hair who dressed in all black. There was some fantasy artwork of a weird dragon-parrot creature on the website's home page. David found a drummer named Scott Harrison. It had to be the same guy Alicia mentioned Mia had been dating. He clicked on a web page for upcoming shows. The band was scheduled to play in Houston tonight but were back in Austin for a show tomorrow night.

David wondered if Mia could possibly be with the band right now. He quickly typed out a message to a booking email listed on the website, claimed he was a lawyer representing a major music label, and that he needed to speak with a band member ASAP. David then found what looked like the same Scott Harrison listed on Facebook and sent him a similar direct message. Grabbing his phone, he also called the bar where they were scheduled to play tonight in Houston and left a voice mail in the same vein—he needed someone from the band to call him back right away. He was exhausting every possible avenue to locate Mia Martinez.

David turned and looked out the window over a busy Congress Avenue. He again thought about the man who'd tried to bribe Skater into coming forward and directly lie about Rebel being the shooter. Who was he? David figured he was getting close to the truth, and *someone* was beginning to panic. Who was that someone? And what was that truth? He was juggling so many unknowns.

David spun back toward his desk when his cell phone buzzed. He hoped it might be a return call from one of the many messages he'd just sent out to the band. It wasn't—but it made him perk up just the same. A direct call from the same anonymous phone number who'd given him the news article about Eduardo Martinez and had sent him on the wild-goose chase to the hotel bar yesterday.

He hurried to answer it. "Hello?"

It was quiet on the other end. But he thought he could hear nervous breathing.

"Hello?" he repeated. "You there?"

A timid woman's voice. "Did you find out who the two men were in the hotel bar yesterday?"

"Well, I was actually hoping you could tell me."

"You couldn't identify either guy?"

"Yes, one so far. The lawyer, Barksdale. You know him?"

"What about the other man?"

David figured that she'd so easily dismissed his revelation about Barksdale because she already knew him. There was a connection there that immediately got his mind spinning. "I'm still working on it. Who are you? How did you know about the meeting yesterday?"

"I'd rather not say. I just . . . I don't know what to do right now."

David pondered a possibility. "Mia?"

"Who is Mia?"

David could tell by her flat response that the woman on the other end wasn't Mia Martinez. "No one. Can I get your name?"

A long pause. "Charlotte."

David scribbled down the name on his notepad but questioned its authenticity.

"Are you okay, Charlotte? Are you in some kind of trouble?"

"No, I'm not okay."

"Why?"

"Someone has been following me."

"Why would someone be following you?"

"I think they suspect I know something more about Luke Murphy."

David felt his heart start to race. "Do you?"

She sighed but didn't respond.

"Charlotte, who is *they*? You said *they* suspect."

"I can't sleep," she replied, ignoring his question. "I can hardly eat right now; my stomach is turned in so many knots. This is a nightmare."

"I want to help you, believe me. But I need you to tell me more."

Again, she didn't respond. David was getting frustrated.

"Please talk to me," he begged her. "I can meet you somewhere *right now*."

"I'm sorry, David. I don't think I can do this anymore."

"Wait . . ."

She abruptly hung up. David cursed. But he immediately yanked his laptop closer to him, pulled up the website for Barksdale's law firm, Sewell & Merritt. He clicked on a link for Attorneys and typed in a search for the name *Charlotte*. No one with that first name popped up. David then began scanning individual profiles for each female attorney listed with the firm's Austin office—thirty-seven of them. He'd nearly scanned the full list without finding anyone of interest when he suddenly paused on the face of a twentysomething woman with dark hair and the most engaging green eyes. The mysterious KP. The same woman from the second security video who was with Murphy at the Dirty Dog—and who had followed him into the alley the night of his death. The same woman who had confronted David on the sidewalk outside the county jail.

He'd finally found her. Or she'd found him.

Kate Preston.

THIRTY-SIX

The law firm of Sewell & Merritt occupied the top three floors of the historic Littlefield Building at Sixth and Congress. David waited in the modest lobby of the building that afternoon, hoping for an opportunity to privately engage Kate Preston should she at some point walk out of one of the building's three elevators. He wasn't sure what else to do at this point. He had to somehow convince Kate to talk to him. But she was clearly scared, so David knew he had to be careful about it. He couldn't just take the elevator up to the lobby of Sewell & Merritt and request a meeting with her. Not if one of her colleagues was somehow involved in Murphy's death.

He also couldn't sit around and do nothing. Kate was a central piece to his figuring out what really happened the night that Rebel was in the alley with Murphy. Hell, his entire case might be tied up in what she knew. So he sat in a leather chair in the corner of the small lobby, a magazine up in his face, casually hiding his identity, while surveying the various people who came in and out of the building all afternoon. So far, no Kate Preston. He knew she was currently in the office. He'd called the firm's main number earlier, asked for Kate, and hung up when she answered. His quick research on Kate told him she'd gone to Clemson before getting her law degree from the University of

Virginia. She'd joined Sewell & Merritt straight out of law school just a year ago—right around the same time David had joined Hunter & Kellerman. Kate's profile page said she focused on advising clients on general corporate practice, including mergers and acquisitions. Other online searching showed she'd played soccer while at Clemson, where she'd earned Second Team All-Conference her senior year.

David had also run several online searches trying to somehow group Murphy and Kate together but came up with *nothing*. There was at least no official online record of them doing anything together, workwise or personal. So what was the connection? David again wondered if they could've been having some sort of secret affair. Kate was a very attractive woman. Could that have been the reason she became intertwined in this whole thing? He hoped to find that out—*if* she ever walked out of the elevators.

The Littlefield Building had limited parking, which meant most who worked inside had to park nearby in paid lots or garages. Chances were good that Kate would eventually step out into the lobby. She finally did around five that afternoon. She wore a knee-length black skirt, black heels, and a white blouse covered by a black leather jacket. She seemed to be leaving the building by herself, which was good. David planted his face in his phone, knowing that Kate would recognize him. He didn't want that to happen yet. Not until he was somewhere safer with her where they could talk privately.

David waited until Kate hit the outside doors, then jumped from the chair and quickly followed. The sidewalks were busy with people as numerous surrounding buildings began emptying out for the evening. That made it easy for David to trail Kate without being spotted. She followed the sidewalk up to Congress and then moved north toward the Texas Capitol building. David followed closely behind, wondering where Kate was going. She had her purse with her but no briefcase or bag, which led him to believe she'd be returning to the office. As he knew all too well, a corporate lawyer rarely goes home at this hour.

A large group of people stopped at a crosswalk, waiting for the light to turn. David paused five people behind Kate. He watched as her head pivoted left, right, and back left again, as if she were studying those around her. Who was she looking for? Who would be following her? David jerked back out of view when Kate turned to glance all the way behind her. The walk light appeared, and the mass of people began crossing the street. Kate peeled off and entered Royal Blue Grocery, a small store where downtowners could pick up the essentials. David had been in the store often. He paused at the outside window, took a peek inside. Kate grabbed a small basket and made her way to the back of the store. David figured this was his best chance to engage her. He had no idea what was about to happen but knew he had to start taking calculated risks.

Pushing through the main door, he did a quick scan of the store. Several shoppers were at the checkout counter. A few others were roaming about. None of them seemed to be watching Kate. David took a deep breath, maneuvered through the aisles, found Kate off by herself, picking through various cold sandwich options from a refrigerated shelf. He sidled up next to her.

"Roast beef is their best sandwich," he said, trying to be casual.

She looked over at him.

"Hi, Kate," he said with a small grin.

Her eyes went wide. "What . . . what are you doing here?"

"We need to talk," David whispered.

"How did you find me?"

"I connected a few dots. Please don't freak out."

"I can't do this here."

"Then where?"

Her eyebrows bunched. "I can't do this at all. I already told you that."

"You were with Luke Murphy the night he died. I need to know why."

"How do you know that?"

"I have a security video from one of the bars. It shows you following Murphy into the alley. Right after you were sitting with him at the Dirty Dog."

Kate covered her mouth with a trembling hand. "Who else has seen that?"

"I don't know. Let's just sit down and talk in private."

"I can't."

"Kate, I have a client facing a death sentence here."

"I know . . . I just . . ." Kate peered over toward the front of the store when the main door opened. A man in a brown jacket entered. "I can't, David. I'm sorry. They could be watching us right now."

"Who, Kate? Who is watching us?"

"The same people who killed Luke!"

With that, Kate dropped her basket to the floor, brushed right past David, and hurried toward the front of the store.

"Kate, wait!"

Pulling the main door open, Kate ducked into heavy sidewalk traffic again. David rushed outside behind her, watched in dismay as she darted in and out of the crowd and then completely disappeared.

THIRTY-SEVEN

David huddled with Thomas back at the office that evening.

"She just ran away?" his partner asked him.

"Basically. She refused to talk to me."

"I thought you were good with the ladies."

"Not this one."

Standing at his office window, David watched as the sun set on the city. He'd already tried to call the phone number Kate had used to contact him, but the phone was no longer in service. Kate had apparently shut it down. It was a bad sign if she was now severing all communication with him.

Thomas sat in a guest chair and scanned photos on David's cell phone of Barksdale and the other man sitting at the hotel bar.

"You still have no idea about this other guy?" Thomas asked.

David turned, shrugged. "No clue. He's not a lawyer over at Sewell and Merritt. I've searched their entire database. And Kate acted like she didn't know him. She clearly wanted to know who he was, so he must be connected to all of this somehow. I've thought about confronting Barksdale directly. But if Kate is truly in some kind of danger, I don't want to do something stupid."

"I know a couple of guys over at Sewell and Merritt. Maybe I could show them this photo and see if anything turns up."

"It's worth a shot," David replied. "I'm kind of desperate here."

"So are others, it seems. You know how I've been getting the runaround with the city about gaining access to their camera footage? Well, there's a reason behind it. They've been instructed from the top to stall and redirect."

"How do you know that?"

"I just got off the phone with a guy who works in the city's Public Information Office. Our daughters play soccer together. I told him my situation at practice the other day, and he said he'd look into it for me. He called to tell me a buddy of his who works directly with the cameras privately told him about the stalling. Said although it didn't come down through any official channels, it was made clear to everyone by their superiors that they were to not play nice with us. We were even addressed by name."

"Are you serious? Can he find out who was behind these instructions?"

"I'm not going to push. I could tell he wasn't too comfortable even sharing this info with me. He didn't want to get himself or anyone else in trouble. What the hell is going on here, David? We've got someone breaking into our office in the middle of the night and busting you up real good. And probably the same guy out on the streets, trying to bribe a homeless kid into lying in court. We've got Dana telling you the DA is getting pressure from the outside to get rid of this case. And now city employees are being told to hide pertinent information from us?"

"Sounds like you've finally jumped into the conspiracy boat with me."

"Yeah, I'm definitely in the boat now. But I don't like it one bit."

"Me, neither. I've got to find Mia Martinez."

THIRTY-EIGHT

David's phone buzzed by his ear, waking him. The dog was curled up at his feet on the sofa, snoring away. David rolled over, found his phone, stared at the screen with blurry eyes. Two thirty? It was a local number but not anyone in his phone contacts.

He answered with a curt "What?"

There was no response. He pulled the phone away from his ear, looked to see if he had a signal. Everything seemed okay.

"Who is this?" he asked, his eyes barely staying open.

Sandy kicked at him, growing more annoyed by the interruption. David could hear nervous breathing. Someone was there. Could it be . . . ?

"Kate?" he whispered.

"That was a really dumb thing you did," she said.

He sat up, swung his bare feet to the floor, the fog quickly clearing. The dog perked up, tilted his head at David.

"I'm sorry. I really am. But I didn't know what else to do."

"You could've gotten me into big trouble."

"Big trouble with who, Kate? Please talk to me."

"Not over the phone."

David felt a glimmer of hope. "Okay. Where?"

"Are you prepared to play by my rules from here on out?"

"Whatever you say."

"I'm serious, David. No more showing up uninvited. No more surprises. You do it my way, or I'm out. Do you understand?"

"Yes, I do. I promise."

"Meet me at the Stevie Ray Vaughan statue on the running trail."

"When?"

"Right now. Do you have a baseball cap?"

"Sure. Several."

"Wear a cap backward."

"Seriously?"

"Do you want me to hang up?"

"Okay, okay. Backward cap. Stevie Ray Vaughan statue. Anything else?"

"Just wait there. I'll find you."

The statue memorialized the late blues guitarist in his perpetual flat-brimmed hat, poncho, and holding a guitar by his side. It was an Austin landmark on the south side of Lady Bird Lake, the stretch of the Colorado River that weaves its way through the city. David stood right next to Stevie, hands plunged deep in his blue jean pockets, his black Abilene Christian University baseball cap sitting backward on his head as instructed.

David looked both ways up and down the trail but saw no sign of Kate yet. The running trail was empty. It was the dead middle of the night. He turned and watched as the lights from the downtown skyline reflected like glitter off the calm water. He could see the Frost Bank Tower poking up in the middle of all the buildings. The walk to the statue was an easy five blocks for David. Was it also a walk for Kate? Did she live downtown? Was she at her office when she called him? He had so many questions and hoped to have some answers soon. He picked up a couple of rocks, skipped them off the water. He waited ten long minutes, and still no sign of Kate. He was starting to worry she was not going to show when he heard her voice behind him.

"David?"

He turned. Her dark hair was tucked under an Astros baseball cap. She wore jeans, running shoes, and the same gray hoodie she'd had on the first night they'd met on the sidewalk outside the county jail—when he thought she might be on drugs or just a crazy person. Not an attorney.

"Hey," he said.

She cast a nervous glance over her shoulder. "Let's be quick, okay?"

"Whatever you say. You make the rules."

They shared a brief grin. "You'll understand in a moment."

"I hope so."

She walked past him toward the water. "How did you find me today?"

"I suspected you might work with Lee Barksdale at Sewell and Merritt because you didn't seem that surprised when I mentioned his name on the phone. So I did a search of the firm's website and recognized you from the other night outside the jail. Then I waited for you in the lobby."

"I see."

"Who is Charlotte?" he asked.

She turned, another small smile. "First name that came to me yesterday. My favorite children's book."

"*Charlotte's Web*?"

She nodded. "Yeah."

"Great book," David agreed.

A shadowy figure appeared way down the trail from them, clearly making Kate uncomfortable.

"Let's walk," she suggested.

They circled around Stevie and headed up the trail, away from the figure, walking in and around dark tree shadows, staying close to the water's edge.

Kate began telling her story. "About ten days ago, I'm sitting inside a conference room with my colleague Lee, and we're working on a client transactional matter. He steps out of the room for a moment to go deal with something—I don't remember what exactly—and he leaves his phone sitting out on the conference table, right in front of me amid the piles of paperwork. A text pops up on his screen from someone his phone identifies simply as Nelly. I only glanced at the text because it was a photo of a young guy with this teardrop tattoo under his right eye. Below the text was this message from the sender: *This is the guy. Eduardo Martinez. Coordinate with Jake, and take care of this ASAP.* I thought nothing more of it until the next day when I'm on the treadmill at the gym, watching the late local news. I see a photo of the same guy with the teardrop tattoo suddenly appear on my TV screen, and the anchor is saying how Martinez was shot dead earlier that night. Considering the text message on Lee's phone, this news *really* disturbed me."

"What did you do?"

"I wasn't sure what to do. I thought of asking Lee about it, but I don't really know the guy that well. And how do you even broach a subject like this with someone? I thought of contacting the police, but it felt premature without knowing if there was something more to it. Going to the police could cause a lot of drama for me around the office, and if it turned out to be nothing, it would certainly put me in a bad position with the partners. So I tried to just forget about the whole thing. Pretend it never happened."

"I guess that didn't work."

"No, not at all. I couldn't sleep for two nights in a row. Not a wink. I just stared at the ceiling all night, wondering if I was working right next to a guy who had something to do with the murder of another man. So I privately reached out to someone over at the DA's office to see if he could help me."

"Murphy?"

She nodded. "I met Luke Murphy at a legal seminar a few months ago. I reminded him who I was, then told him about my situation. He offered to do some checking around on the case and get back to me."

"So there was nothing more to your relationship with Murphy?"

"What do you mean?"

"The bartender at the Dirty Dog implied y'all were acting a bit cozy."

Her forehead bunched. "How did you even find out I was at the bar with him that night?"

"He scribbled down a meeting in his day planner with the initials *KP*. I thought he might be having an affair with you."

"No, it was nothing like that. We were only sitting closely together so we could talk privately. I suggested that bar because I knew none of my colleagues would likely show up there. I didn't want anyone from the office even asking me about him. I was just being careful. For good reason, I now know."

"What did Murphy tell you?"

"He said I was right to be suspicious. He'd talked to a few police contacts and what he said were other important sources. Although he didn't give me any details, Luke believed that something bigger may be in play. He said he was going to keep investigating and get back to me again. Then he left."

"But you went after him?"

She nodded. "Only because he forgot his credit card at the bar. So I hurried after him and spotted him cutting into that alley . . ." Kate covered her mouth with a shaky hand.

"What happened, Kate? What did you see?"

She swallowed. "Another man I didn't notice at first had gone into the alley right behind him. I was about to call out to Luke, get him to stop so I could return the credit card, when this other man suddenly pulled out a gun and shot him in the back of the head." Her eyes began watering up. "I couldn't believe it. It all happened so fast. This guy didn't even say anything to Luke. He just aimed the gun and shot him."

"Did you get a look at the guy?"

She shook her head. "Not really. It was dark. I didn't see his face, but he had a hat on and a green jacket. When he noticed me, I completely freaked and ran out of the alley, terrified I would also be shot. Later that night, I saw on the news that the police had arrested a homeless man suspected in Luke's death. They were calling it a random act of violence, but I knew they were wrong."

"If you didn't get a good look at the guy, how do you know it wasn't my client who actually pulled the trigger?"

"Because I saw your client leaning up against the building not two seconds before the shooting."

"You did?"

"I don't know why I just glanced over at him. He was sitting upright, but it looked like he was sleeping."

David's heart started to pound. "Are you sure, Kate?"

"Yes. When they showed his mug shot on TV, I knew it was the same guy. Your client didn't shoot Luke. Someone else did."

David felt a flood of relief pour through him. Although he'd willed himself to believe it, hearing the truth was exhilarating. Rebel was truly innocent.

"Why didn't you go to the police?" David asked.

"Luke involved the police and ended up shot dead in the alley."

"Right. So you reached out to me?"

She nodded. "I had to do *something*. At first, I was hoping I could somehow help you find the truth on your own without getting myself more involved. That was naive, I guess, but I didn't know what else to do."

Listening to Kate, David realized this was much bigger than he'd even thought. Anyone who touched this thing could be in serious danger. They had to be more careful, or they might both be killed.

"You used a burner phone to contact me?" he asked.

"Yes, I bought it at Target. But I called you on my real phone tonight."

"Don't do that again, okay? Get another burner. Just to be safe."

"Okay. What do we do now?"

"What does the guy look like who's been following you?"

"Bald, scruffy beard, about your size. Probably late twenties. I've seen him several times this past week. Standing behind me at the bank. Watching me from outside restaurants. Walking down the sidewalks. A scary-looking guy."

"Black combat boots?"

Her brow wrinkled. "Yeah, I think so. How did you know that?"

David sighed. "I suspect the same guy broke into my office the other night and attacked me before getting away."

"Really? Who is he, David? What's going on here?"

"I think Murphy was right. We've stepped right into the middle of some kind of dangerous conspiracy. I think whoever shot Murphy in that alley suspected you spotted him, so he tried to cover his tracks. He tried to throw everyone off his trail by framing my client. Rebel was simply in the wrong place at the wrong time and under the worst of conditions."

Kate shook her head. "Lee has been acting weird around me all week. He's clearly involved in this somehow. I think he suspects I may know something. Maybe he got suspicious that I saw the text message in the conference room that day. I can't be sure. But I found him searching my desk yesterday when I came back from lunch. He said he was just looking for a client file, but he was lying. The file was sitting right out in the open on the corner of my desk. There has been this awkward tension with him all week. We're both pretending that nothing is wrong."

"How did you know about his meeting at the hotel bar?"

"We were in the conference room, and Lee got a call. When he pulled his phone out of his pocket to check, I saw it was from the same Nelly contact. Lee answered it right away and exited the room. When he came back, he told me he had to step out of the office for an hour or so. I could tell something was up, so I secretly followed him. When he sat down at the bar with the other guy, I texted you."

"You were there at the hotel?"

She nodded. "I watched the whole thing from the corner."

"You didn't recognize the other guy?"

"No, I don't know him."

"Could he be one of your firm's clients?"

She shrugged. "Maybe. I ran a search on the name *Nelly* but came up with nothing. I also searched the internet, grouping *Nelly* and *Lee* together, but still came up empty-handed. I don't know the nature of the relationship yet."

"Nelly sounds like a nickname. Which might mean Lee is somehow friends with him. But there clearly is *something* more there."

"I need to go back and more thoroughly check all client matters that Lee has been involved with over the past few years. Maybe there's something there that I just haven't found yet."

"Can you do that without drawing attention to yourself?"

"I don't know. I feel like my every move is being watched right now."

"Don't take any unnecessary risks. Send me the list instead, okay?"

She nodded. "I can't believe all of this has happened. Luke Murphy would still be alive if I hadn't pulled him into this situation."

"None of this is your fault." David put his hand on her arm. "You have to stop thinking that way. We'll get through this together. You have to trust me."

"I have to admit I'm glad you found me today—even though I acted angry. Because I don't think I could've survived another day trying to do this all on my own."

THIRTY-NINE

Later that morning, David raced over to the Dell Seton Medical Center at UT after receiving an urgent phone call that Rebel had been badly injured in a late-night jail altercation and had been rushed to the emergency room. There were no other details. David felt fear grip him. Had Rebel been targeted? Was that what the altercation was really about? After his conversation with Kate, David believed it was entirely possible that someone had intentionally tried to take his client out to make this whole case go away.

At the front desk, David found out that his client was in a private post-op room recovering from emergency surgery. He negotiated the maze of elevators and hallways and finally found Rebel's private room. A uniformed police officer was standing outside, guarding the door. David flashed his ID to the officer, explained he was the patient's lawyer, and was allowed inside. David stepped into the room. Rebel was lying bare-chested on the hospital bed with his eyes closed. A nurse was currently checking charts and analyzing different beeping machines. David could see white bandages all up and down his client's left midsection. They looked like they were soaked in red. What the hell had happened?

"Is he okay?" David asked the nurse.

"Are you family?"

"His lawyer."

"He's stable now. Let me get the doctor for you."

The nursed stepped out of the room. David moved in closer to the bed. Rebel's face was really pale, but it was good to see his chest going up and down. The man was alive. David noted that his client's right wrist was cuffed to the hospital bed, as if Rebel might jump up and make a run for it. Frustrated, David moved back into the hallway for a moment to talk to the officer.

"Are the handcuffs really necessary?" David asked.

"I'm just following orders, sir."

"He just got out of surgery. What's he going to do?"

"Sorry. Above my pay grade."

A fortysomething dark-haired doctor in scrubs came over to where David was standing. "You're Mr. North's attorney?"

David nodded. "Yes. What happened, Doc?"

"Well, I can't tell you what all happened at the jail, but I can tell you the nature of your client's injuries. He was stabbed four times in the lower abdominals. The punctures were violent and deep, and he lost a lot of blood. Fortunately, we got him here in time to stop the bleeding and minimize the internal damage."

"What was used to stab him?"

"The entry wounds suggest some kind of small sharp object."

David wondered about the weapon. A knife? If so, who did it?

"But he's going to be okay?" David asked.

"He's not out of the woods yet. We also discovered your client has an irregular heartbeat that could lead to ventricular fibrillation, a serious heart rhythm problem that occurs when the heart beats with rapid, erratic electrical impulses that could result in sudden cardiac arrest. After he recovers from his current situation, we'll need to go back in and implant a device to regulate his heart rhythm so that he's not a ticking time bomb. In more ways than one, Mr. North is very lucky to be alive right now."

After the doctor left, David returned to Rebel's bedside. He sat in a chair next to the bed, waited for his client to finally wake up. About an hour later, Rebel finally opened his eyes.

"What . . . the . . . hell?" Rebel groaned.

David jumped up, leaned over the bed. "Hey, Cowboy."

Rebel blinked, tried to focus. "Where the hell am I, Lawyer?"

"Hospital. You had a rough night. But you're okay."

Rebel glanced down at the bandages on his side, squirmed a bit. "Damn. I hate doctors and hospitals. When can I get out of here?"

"Take it easy," David suggested. "These doctors saved your life. Besides, do you really want to rush back over to the jail?"

Rebel squirmed again. "Good point, Lawyer. Food is probably much better over here, anyway. I feel funny, though."

"Well, they got heavy doses of pain meds running through you."

Rebel looked up. "What about the other guy?"

"What other guy?"

"The dirty snake that ambushed me."

David shook his head. "I don't know yet. Tell me what happened."

"Dude thought he could jump me. But it ain't my first rodeo."

"What dude?"

"I dunno, Lawyer. Some young buck they put in my cell with me last night. A meathead with a crew cut and some racist tattoos. Hardly said a word all night. Then he made a move on me the first time I closed my eyes."

David cocked his head. "He just attacked you for no reason?"

"I guess he had his reasons. But he didn't share them with me." Rebel moved his lips all around like they might be numb. "CIA probably sent him in to take care of their dirty work. But I'm a survivor. Always have been."

Rebel didn't act angry about it. He was probably too doped up on pain meds to care much about anything right now. But David suspected his client was right. Not about the CIA but about someone intentionally placing a thug in Rebel's jail cell to try to take him out. How high up did this conspiracy go? If they could get to his client in his jail cell, they could get to him anywhere. David had to do something to protect Rebel better.

Before it was too late.

FORTY

After leaving the hospital, David drove straight over to Neil Mason's office. He barged inside without even knocking. Mason was behind his desk. Two other men in suits were sitting in guest chairs. They all looked up with wide eyes at David's unexpected interruption.

"We need to talk right now," David demanded.

"Well, come on in, David," Mason scoffed. "Don't mind us."

"Right now. I'm serious."

"You should be serious. Your client hasn't been playing nice."

Mason asked the other two men to give him a moment alone with David. When they left the room, David erupted on the prosecutor.

"What the hell is going on, Neil? Why is my client having to defend his own life while under the care of the county?"

Mason raised a hand. "Hold up, David. I think you got your facts wrong. The report I got this morning was your client was the instigator of last night's attack, screaming about Russians and aliens in the middle of the night, acting like the crazy man we've all seen. Hell, he damn near choked the other inmate to death before guards were able to get in there and pull him off. I'd probably be conjuring up new charges for your client right now if I wasn't already throwing the book at him. So go bark elsewhere."

"Someone is lying. I don't believe them."

"I don't care."

"Where did the weapon come from?"

"Beats me. Inmates can be crafty."

"Who's the other guy?"

Mason shrugged. "Just Joe Schmo, in for his second round of assault charges. But according to your client, he's a Russian agent."

"I want to see the guy's file. Better yet, I want to talk to him."

"Good luck with that. I think he's in a coma right now."

"What about video? All the cells are monitored by cameras, right?"

"Correct," Mason admitted.

"Have you even watched video of the incident?"

"I have no reason to doubt trusted county employees. Besides, I have more important legal matters in front of me this morning."

"Well, I don't. I want to see the video ASAP."

Mason sighed, rolled his eyes. He reached over, punched a button on his office phone, and asked his assistant to get him video of the jail incident.

"You happy now?" Mason asked.

"Not yet."

Mason crossed his arms, leaned back in his chair. "The pressure is starting to get to you, isn't it?"

"No. But it's clearly getting to someone."

"Look, murder cases aren't for everyone. There's no shame in admitting that. There's plenty of other good legal work out there for you. These are high stakes."

"I like high stakes."

"Tell that to your face right now," Mason sneered. He stood, circled around to the front of his desk, leaned up against it with a heavy sigh. "You know, David, I talked to Murphy's widow again yesterday. Let me tell you, she's a brokenhearted, grieving woman right now. It would be a real shame to put her through every detail of this horrific tragedy again in a few months. Make her sit there and stare at photos of her husband with his head blown apart. Hell, you've seen them. Those photos are just brutal. What if I put the deal back on the table? Give you another chance to do the right thing."

"What are you trying to hide, Neil?"

"Don't be ridiculous. Tell you what: I'll even drop it to twelve years—your client could be out in six. But you have to say yes right now, here in my office."

David's eyes narrowed. "Who wants this to go away?"

"The people who actually care about Murphy's family, that's all. I thought you were one of them, but I guess I was wrong."

"There's more to this, and you know it."

Mason's office phone beeped and interrupted them. It was his assistant. "Sir, there's no video. Tech says the cameras went down in that whole wing yesterday. They're still working on getting them back online this morning."

David watched as Mason did the slightest of head pitches. It wasn't much—but it was enough to let David know that the prosecutor was surprised to hear that news.

"Thank you, Alice." Mason turned, shrugged. "Sorry. Cameras were down."

"Imagine that. I want my client better protected."

"Protected from whom?"

"From whoever is pressuring you to make a deal so this will all go away."

"You're seriously going to turn down this ludicrous deal?"

"Damn right," David said, headed for the door. "My client is innocent."

Mason yelled after him. "The only protection your client needs right now is from his stubborn lawyer who is going to get him killed!"

FORTY-ONE

David was on the sidewalk right outside the DA's building, still fuming about his tense exchange with Mason, when someone called out his name from behind. He turned, spotted Dana hustling up to him.

Brushing past him, she said, "Follow me. We need to talk."

David trailed her around the corner of the building, where Dana found a hideaway near a set of dumpsters. The pavement was littered with cigarette butts. Looked like a popular place for smoke breaks for county employees, although no one was standing there and lighting up at the moment.

"Your boss is an ass, Dana," David said.

"I already know that."

"Someone tried to have Rebel killed in his jail cell last night. But no one in your office seems to even care about it."

"I believe you, okay? So shut up already."

"You do?"

She glanced behind her, leaned in even closer, and spoke just above a whisper. "I left the office after midnight last night. When I walked into the parking garage, I spotted Jordan standing by his car up the ramp, talking privately with Mayor Nelson. Then Nelson jumps into his Cadillac, spins the tires, and races out of there like a madman."

"They see you?"

She shook her head. "I stayed back by the elevators."

"What were they talking about?"

"I don't know. But the mayor looked pissed."

David arched an eyebrow. "You think the pressure is coming from the mayor?"

"I'm suspicious. Three hours later Rebel got attacked."

David cursed. "Why would the mayor care about Murphy's case?"

"I don't have a clue at this point."

"Do you know a lawyer over at Sewell and Merritt named Lee Barksdale?"

"Doesn't ring a bell. Why?"

"He's involved in this somehow. Murphy was doing an offline investigation about the murder of a guy named Eduardo Martinez, who worked on a city maintenance crew. He ever mention anything to you?"

"No, he didn't."

"Well, I think someone killed him because of it."

"Eduardo Martinez?"

"Yeah, he was killed about a week ago in a so-called drug deal. But I don't think that's what really happened."

"Let me look into it."

"Maybe you shouldn't, Dana."

"Why?"

"Because Murphy looked into it and got himself killed. Because I got attacked in my office. Because Rebel is barely alive this morning. Whoever is behind all of this is starting to get really desperate. I don't want to lose another friend."

"Look, if Jordan is truly corrupt, I'm not going to be caught on a ship that's about to go down around here. You expect me to just sit on my hands?"

David knew there was no way to talk her out of it. Dana was more strong-willed than anyone he'd ever known. "Just promise me you'll be careful, okay?"

"I promise."

FORTY-TWO

David pulled his truck to a stop in front of a small white brick house in a quaint South Austin neighborhood. The yard was well maintained with colorful flower beds. Two tricycles sat in the driveway. A blue ribbon had been tied around the only tree in the front yard. David took a deep breath, let it out very slowly. He'd been to Murphy's house only once before, when he'd first moved to town. Murphy had grilled steaks for them in the backyard. Since then, every time he and Murphy had gotten together, it was at a sports bar to hang out, watch games, and drink beer.

David grabbed the flowers he'd purchased on the way over and got out of his vehicle. With each step toward the front door, he felt his heart pound a bit heavier. He took another deep breath, then knocked. He could hear a toddler singing somewhere inside the house. Seconds later, he spotted Michelle Murphy's face in the side window. Then he heard the door lock being unfastened, and she opened the door.

Michelle was a pretty blonde who usually had high energy. But today she wore no makeup, her eyes were red and hollow, and her shoulders sagged under a long-sleeve flannel shirt.

For a moment, neither of them said anything.

David could feel his heart in his throat. "Is it okay that I'm here?"

She nodded, swallowed. "Of course."

"Are you sure, Michelle? Because I can turn around right now and drive away if you're angry with me."

"I'm not angry. Just . . . confused. I don't have the energy for much else."

"I wanted to come sooner. I've just been trying to find the right moment."

"Please, come in, David."

Opening the door, Michelle led him inside the house. She thanked him for the flowers, set them on a dining table that was already covered with other flower arrangements. David glanced into the living room, where Murphy's two small kids were playing with toys on the floor. The three-year-old boy was the spitting image of Murphy. The two-year-old girl looked more like Michelle. David felt it surreal to be standing there, looking at those kids, knowing their father would never be coming home to them again. He felt his eyes grow wet.

"You want some coffee?" Michelle offered. "Or lemonade? That's about all I have right now."

"No, I'm good. Thank you. Can we talk?"

She led him into a small study with a desk and two brown leather guest chairs that had been Murphy's home office. David immediately spotted a framed photo on the bookshelf of him and Murphy wearing softball uniforms, arms over each other's shoulders, acting like two idiots. It was taken at a law school softball tournament. David remembered Murphy had driven home the winning run that day. For fun, David had poured a bucket of blue Gatorade over him. Staring at the picture, David felt a new wave of grief hit him hard. He realized he hadn't even taken a moment to properly mourn the death of his friend because he'd been so busy with the case. But now was also not the time.

Sitting down with Michelle, David didn't have the first clue where to start, so he chose the children. "How're the kids?"

"I don't think it's real to them yet, even though we've tried to explain it. Ashlie asked me last night when Daddy was coming home."

"Do you need any help around here? I'm pretty good with a tool set."

She gave him a small smile. "That's not how I remember it, David. Justin's crib was a total disaster."

They shared a quick laugh. Back at Stanford, David had gone over to Murphy's apartment to help build a crib for the expectant baby boy. Michelle was eight months' pregnant. He and Murphy drank too much while doing it, and the crib fell completely apart when Michelle tried to put the bedding in place. The boys had laughed their heads off, but Michelle had been pissed at them.

"I blame Murphy," David said. "He broke out that bottle of Garrison Brothers bourbon way too early."

Another shared smile. Then more awkward silence. It was so hard to believe he was sitting there with Michelle under these circumstances.

"What am I going to do without him, David?" Michelle said.

"What you've always done. Roll your sleeves up and get to work. You're one of the strongest women I've ever been around."

"Not strong enough to handle this by myself."

"You'll never be by yourself. We'll be here for you."

She pressed her lips together. "It's really good to see you."

"I'm sorry it's taken me this long."

"I was actually going to call you today, anyway."

David raised an eyebrow. "You were?"

"Jeff Jordan called me this morning. He said the DA's office had made a very generous plea offer to you in hopes they could avoid a trial and spare me from having to relive all of this. He asked if I would be willing to call you and try to talk some sense into you. I just hadn't gotten around to doing it yet."

David thought about the exchange between Jordan and Mayor Gregory Nelson last night and Mason's unexpected new offer this morning. Now they were manipulating Michelle? He felt anger bubbling up below the surface. "Listen to me, Michelle. You've known me for a lot of years now. You know how much I loved your husband. Murphy always had my back. And now I've got to have Murphy's back, too."

Michelle wrinkled her nose. "What . . . what do you mean?"

David decided to not dance around the truth. "Murphy was not killed in some random shooting by a homeless guy. Your husband was killed because he'd begun a private investigation that I believe threatened to somehow expose some powerful people."

Her brow bunched. "That's not what they've told me."

"I think certain people at the DA's office could possibly be involved."

Her eyes widened. "What? How do you know this?"

"I've spent the past few days discovering a lot of what Murphy had uncovered."

Michelle ran her fingers through her hair. "I can't handle this, David. I just can't. I don't even want to know anything more about it. It takes everything within me to get from hour to hour with my kids right now."

"I understand. But you needed to hear it straight from me."

She nodded. "Okay."

"Did Murphy keep any files at home? Did he have a private lockbox or anything like that around here where he might have kept important paperwork?"

She pointed toward a set of cabinets behind the desk. "He kept some files in that drawer over there. I think it's mostly our personal financials and stuff. You're welcome to take a look. I don't care."

The kids started fighting about a toy in the next room, so Michelle excused herself to go deal with it. Walking over to the cabinet, David pulled a drawer out and began rummaging through Murphy's home files. Just like Michelle had suggested, most of it was personal files for their bank records, taxes, bills, mortgage info, car info, and so forth.

There didn't appear to be anything in the drawer that was work related. David searched the desk drawers next. Again, he found mainly miscellaneous personal items, office supplies, and the sort. When he opened the middle drawer, he found a clear Ziploc bag containing Murphy's wedding ring, his watch, his money clip still stuffed with cash, and his cell phone.

"A policeman dropped that by a few days ago," Michelle said, standing at the door of the study. "I stuck it in the drawer and haven't even touched it."

David pulled the cell phone out of the bag. "Do you mind if I take a look?"

She shrugged. "If you think it might help you."

"Do you know his password?"

Michelle gave it to him. In the next room, Ashlie was yelling for Mommy again, so Michelle excused herself. When the phone powered up, David typed in the password and stared at a screen with all the usual apps, along with dozens of kid-friendly ones that Murphy probably had used to entertain his children. David first clicked on Email. He was surprised to find Murphy's email completely empty. David did the same with the calendar. He found no date entries listed. When David opened up Messages, he discovered the exact same thing. Empty. No emails, no messages, no voice mails. Everything had been wiped clean.

Was that intentional? Had someone made sure to scrub Murphy's phone before giving it back to Michelle? Not everything had been deleted. David scrolled through hundreds of photos—most of which were of the kids—and several times he had to push back waves of grief. He reviewed a couple of organizational apps but again found nothing that caught his attention. Remembering that the security video had shown Murphy to be on his phone when he'd entered the alley, David went back to the Phone app again. Although there were no longer any stored voice mail messages, he did discover that the call log was still intact—it had not been deleted. He quickly scanned a list of the most recent incoming and outgoing calls.

There were no calls from the past week, of course, since the phone was likely shut off after being confiscated at the crime scene. But there was a phone call Murphy had placed that matched up with the exact time stamp for when he'd left the Dirty Dog the night of his death.

When Murphy was killed, he was on the phone with DA Jordan.

David cursed quietly, his mouth dropping open. Why had this not been disclosed to him? What had Murphy said to his boss that night? This information was critical to the case. They couldn't just make it disappear. David swallowed. Or could they? Jordan and Mayor Nelson were two of the most powerful political figures in the city. If this thing went as high up as David was starting to think, where would he turn for help?

FORTY-THREE

David rushed back to the office and found Bobby E. Lee sitting in a chair outside the main office door per usual. The old man in the gray soldier uniform stood and saluted. David had tried and failed many times over the past six months to get him to stop doing it. Now he just rolled with it like it was normal.

"Morning, Bobby."

"Mr. Adams?" Bobby Lee said, surprising David. The man rarely said a word to him.

David turned. "Yes?"

Bobby Lee reached down beside the chair, grabbed a standard white envelope off the dusty floor. "A gentleman dropped this off for you a few minutes ago. He asked me to give it to you and *only* you."

David took the envelope. "You get a name?"

"I asked. He wouldn't say."

"All right, thanks."

David walked into his office and circled around to his desk. His mind was still racing a mile a minute about the phone call Murphy had placed to Jordan just seconds before his death. Did Mason know about this call? If he did and had intentionally chosen not to disclose it, David was going to give him hell. David dropped into his office chair, stared at the envelope Bobby Lee had just given him. It was sealed with no writing on the outside. Tearing it open, he found nothing but a small flash drive inside. David stuck the device into his laptop, hoping he wasn't about to load a virus onto his computer, and watched as a digital folder appeared on the screen. It contained a single video icon with no title.

Clicking "Play," he watched the screen as the video appeared. David perked up suddenly. The video looked like it was taken from a security camera inside of one of the county jail cells. Was this from last night? He leaned in even closer to his laptop. A date-and-time stamp in the upper right-hand corner confirmed it was captured at exactly 3:32 a.m. The jail cell had two beds on opposite sides of the small room with a wall sink separating them. Both beds were occupied by inmates. It sure as hell looked like his client in the bed on the left. In the other bed was a muscle-bound guy covered in tattoos with a brown Mohawk.

Seconds after the video began, the big guy with the Mohawk slipped out of his bed while holding something small in his right hand. He quickly moved toward the other bed, jumped on top of Rebel, and began thrusting at him with his right hand. David felt his heart racing. Rebel screamed out in pain, but he immediately responded to the attack with a vicious right-hand chop that struck the big guy in the neck. Just as quick, Rebel's left palm thrust upward and popped the guy square in his nose, causing the guy to holler and fall back onto the hard floor. The guy grasped at his neck, as if he couldn't breathe, while blood from his nose began to pour all over his face. In a split second, Rebel was out of the bed and on top of the guy, his hands clutched around the man's neck. A jail deputy then burst into the cell, where he tried to pull Rebel off. Two more deputies quickly arrived. Then the video went black.

David again pressed "Play," watched the video a second time through. He was shocked at how easily his client had defended himself from such a vicious sneak attack by a powerful-looking man. Two swift moves by Rebel—one with the right hand, one with the left—and he'd rendered a hulking man nearly powerless. And his client had done it while almost bleeding to death. Where had he learned to do that?

David jumped out of his chair and rushed back into the hallway.

"Tell me again who gave you the envelope, Bobby."

Bobby Lee's forehead bunched. "Everything okay, Mr. Adams?"

"Yes, I just need to know more about the man who dropped this off with you. What exactly did he look like?"

"Well, let's see now. He had a crew cut, like a military guy."

"About how old would you say?"

Bobby Lee shrugged. "I dunno for sure. Maybe fifty."

"You remember what he was wearing?"

"He had on a black jacket, like a jogger's jacket. And he wore brown glasses."

David's brow furrowed. "Square-shaped glasses?"

"Yes, sir. You know him?"

"Maybe."

David flashed on the face of Keith Carter. Could the man have possibly obtained the security video? Carter had mentioned having insider friends, but this felt like a big leap. Mason had flat-out denied the security video even existed. So how would Carter have gotten his hands on it? More so, how would Carter have known David wanted the video?

"Anything else you can remember, Bobby? This is *really* important."

"No, sir, that's about it. He was here only for a few seconds. He walked up to me, handed me the envelope, said what he said, real polite and all, and then he turned around and left. And that was that."

Returning to his office, David sat down at his desk and searched his top drawer for the business card Carter had given him the other day for the Texas Veterans Legal Assistance Project. He had no idea where he put it, so he just searched Google for the main phone number. A woman answered on the second ring.

"VLAP, this is Cindy. How can I help you?"

"Hi, Cindy, I need to talk with Keith Carter. Is he in the office? Or can I get his cell phone from you?"

"Who?"

"Keith Carter," David repeated.

"I'm sorry, sir, but I don't know anyone by that name who works in this office."

"What do you mean? He gave me a business card for the Texas Veterans Legal Assistance Project."

"Really? Well, I'm new here. But I don't see his name on my directory sheet."

"Is this the only office?"

"Yes, for the entire state. Do you want me to ask around and call you back?"

"Yes, please."

David gave her his number, hung up, and rubbed his chin. When it dawned on him where he may have stuck the business card, he took his jacket off a coatrack and began searching the pockets. Carter's card was in the front left pocket. He stared at the phone number. It was different from the one he'd just called.

Grabbing his phone, he called the number on the card but reached Carter's voice mail greeting: "This is Keith Carter with the Texas Veterans Legal Assistance Project. Please leave a message, and I'll get right back to you." When the voice mail message beeped, David said, "Carter, this is David Adams. Call me back ASAP. It's important."

Hanging up, he stared a hole into the business card and tried to make sense of the phone call with VLAP's main office. Was the woman simply mistaken? Did she miss Carter's name on the directory? Or was something else going on? Sitting down, David did a quick search on his laptop for *Keith Carter* and *VLAP*. Nothing popped up with the two together. That was weird. David did a second search using the words *Keith Carter, University of Houston*. There were hundreds of mentions of a Carter, a Keith, or both tied to the University of Houston—but not a single one of them was specifically for an English professor named Keith Carter. He'd told David he'd taught at the university for twenty years. David did one last search: *Keith Carter, Richmond Flying Squirrels*. He scrolled down the entire first page of results. Strike three—there was nothing online that showed someone named Keith Carter had ever played minor-league baseball in Richmond, Virginia.

David sat all the way back in his chair, his mind spinning in a hundred different directions. It seemed as if Keith Carter was a complete fabrication.

Why? Who was this guy, really? And why was he helping David?

FORTY-FOUR

David greeted Theodore Billings in the entry room of the office. The young TV reporter with the plastered-on black hair wore clothes similar to what he'd worn the other day when they'd met—oversize khaki pants and a white button-down shirt with the sleeves rolled up. David ushered him into his own office, shut the door behind them. Billings set a bag of video gear on the floor.

"Thanks for coming so quickly," David said.

"What's the deal with the old man sitting out in the hallway?"

"He's my private security detail."

Billings raised his eyebrows. "Really?"

"I'll explain later. Let's get to this first."

"All righty."

"You need my help getting set up?"

"Nah, just give me a minute."

The reporter unzipped the bag, pulled out a video camera, a stand, some lighting equipment, and then set everything up around David's desk.

"When will this air?" David asked.

"I'll head straight back to the station from here, quickly edit the footage, and turn the story into my boss. It's high interest, so I know he'll want to put it in the local news loop right away. *If* everything checks out."

"It will. I need this out there ASAP."

"I hear you." Billings pulled out a small notepad. "Let's review what you told me over the phone. You said your client was viciously attacked last night by another inmate while at the county jail?"

"Correct. Stabbed four times and rushed to the emergency room."

"Is he stable?"

"Yes, but he's fortunate to be alive."

"And you believe the attack was planned?"

"Yes. The guy was purposely put into the cell with my client. Which is why I need my client better protected."

"Better protected while at the hospital?"

"Yes. I have reason to believe he's still in grave danger. But I'm getting no movement at all from the other side."

"So you want to use me to put pressure on them?"

"You have a problem with that?"

"Nope. But, tell me, who wants your client dead? That's a big story."

"That's for another day, Teddy."

"Fair enough. You should know I talked with a jail spokesman on the way over here. He directly contradicted your version of what happened. He claims your client instigated the whole encounter with the other inmate, who was only defending himself. He puts the blame for your client's current condition solely on him."

"He's lying."

"That's a bold statement. Do you have proof?"

David turned his laptop to face the reporter and played the security video that showed Rebel being attacked by the other man.

Billings's eyes widened as the scene unfolded. "Damn, you're right." He looked up at David. "Why would they lie to me about what happened when you have a video of the whole incident?"

"They don't know I have the video."

"Seriously?"

"They told me their cameras were down."

"So where did you get it?"

"Not important."

"Okay, but can I use it in this news segment?"

"I have a copy ready for you."

Billings grinned ear to ear. "Let's get started."

FORTY-FIVE

David spent the entire afternoon huddled inside his office, door locked, blinds drawn. He even asked Bobby Lee to sit right outside his office door and let no one bother him. The old man took the assignment seriously and even barked at Thomas a few times. Kate had texted him a long list of all client matters that Lee Barksdale had worked on the past five years. David could feel the momentum building as they put more pieces of the puzzle together. There were stacks of paper all over his desk where he'd printed out various online articles and media reports he'd found about companies tied to legal matters on Barksdale's list. It was an exhausting process searching companies one at a time and looking for any threads that might connect to Murphy's death. So far, he'd found nothing that stood out. His mind was growing fuzzy, and his vision was blurred after five straight hours of staring at his computer screen.

David was starting to lose hope when he typed in the name of a commercial real estate group called Lion Partners. A photo appeared on his screen of the founding partner. David immediately sat up straighter in his chair, pulled his laptop closer to him. The guy had a goatee, wore glasses, and was prematurely balding on top. Nelly? The same man Barksdale had met with at the hotel bar the other day. David squinted at the screen. The man's real name was Owen Nelson.

David did a quick double take. Nelson? Could there be a direct connection? He quickly typed in both *Owen Nelson* and *Mayor Gregory Nelson*. Another photo appeared on the screen of the two men standing together at a recent opening of a new downtown building. David's mouth dropped open. The caption claimed Owen Nelson was the mayor's oldest son. David immediately thought of Mayor Nelson in the parking garage, getting pissed at DA Jordan before racing off. All of it had to be tied together.

David felt a renewed surge of energy. He ran a search grouping *Owen Nelson* with *Lee Barksdale* and discovered an LSU alumni site with pictures of the two men together from several years back—along with a group of other college-age guys who were all part of the same fraternity. As suspected, Barksdale and Nelson were more than just business acquaintances—they were old friends. David searched more on Nelson's company, Lion Partners, and found it to be very active in new downtown development opportunities. But its biggest project by far was a $1 billion proposal for a new mixed-use complex called Parker Place, with three new towers for condos, businesses, retail outlets, and restaurants. It was being hailed as Austin's largest-ever private development. The project had been repeatedly delayed the past few years—mostly because of financial setbacks. But Parker Place had gained serious traction of late because Lion Partners had finally secured a new global partner—with direct help from the mayor.

David practically stuck his nose to his laptop screen. Mayor Nelson's fingerprints were all over the project. He'd been championing it since the beginning and had been intricately involved in courting out-of-town financial partners with deep pockets. Most of the news articles said the project would've never gotten this far down the road without the mayor's influence and involvement.

David dropped back into his chair. Could Eduardo Martinez have known something that might have jeopardized this project in some way? Something that Murphy also discovered that got him killed, too?

If so, what? Martinez was just a city maintenance worker, which was about as low on the ladder of political influence as one could get. It didn't make sense that he could have known something so potent that it put his life at risk. Having said that, the pressure the mayor was putting on the DA to make the case go away was real. To the point where Mason was offering David a deal that seemed ludicrous.

David stared at the ceiling. Could the mayor really be involved with murder? He was having a difficult time wrapping his head around that possibility.

Still—$1 billion was *a lot* of money.

FORTY-SIX

David met Dana next to the Texas African American History Memorial on the pristine grounds of the Capitol an hour later. She had texted David a few minutes earlier, said it was urgent, asked to meet ASAP. He could tell she was anxious by the way she had her arms crossed and was constantly shifting her weight back and forth. She used to have the same fidgets and posture right before a big mock trial at Stanford.

"Hey, what do you got?" he said, stepping in close to her.

"I was going back through Murphy's online files, like I told you I would, seeing if anything new stood out. I again didn't find anything upon first glance, just like when I did this same exercise a week ago. All of his online files are attached to cases I already know all about. But then I decided to do a search by date and time, just to see if Murphy had opened up a new file with *any* of his cases on the day he was killed. Well, he did. He created a new file under his McManus case just a few hours before he died."

"McManus?"

"Standard case," Dana explained. "Ethan McManus. Assault with a deadly weapon. His lawyer says it was self-defense. Murphy had been working on it for a few weeks. The new file he'd created was labeled

Neighbor Testimony. However, there was no testimony inside. Actually, what I found wasn't even connected to the McManus case at all."

David inched even closer. "What was in the file?"

A group of tourists made their way to the memorial, talking loudly and snapping photos. Dana pulled David around to the back to talk in private.

"He'd uploaded a set of photos," Dana explained. "The pics are all of a city work crew. About five guys doing construction, wearing the standard yellow vests with *City of Austin* printed on them. It looks like they were building a big gazebo behind someone's house."

She held up her phone to show David the images. She paused on a photo of the address plate set in the brick on the outside of the home.

"Whose house?" David asked.

"Gregory and Margaret Nelson."

David raised an eyebrow. "This is the mayor's house?"

Dana nodded. "I think Murphy intentionally mislabeled the file to hide these pics because he suspected corruption." She held up her phone again. "Look closer—in the reflection of the window. Recognize him?"

David squinted. At first, he hadn't noticed, but he could now clearly see a reflection of the photographer in the window next to the house's address plate.

"Eduardo Martinez."

"Yep. It at least appears in these photos that the mayor was personally using Martinez's work crew to build a backyard gazebo."

"Is that legal?" David asked.

"No, not if it's on the taxpayers' dime."

"You think Martinez somehow knew that and took the pics to extort the situation?"

"It fits. But where did Murphy get these pics?"

"From Mia Martinez," David said, putting it together. "She had to have given these photos to Murphy the day he was killed."

"I don't know. Are we really standing here talking about implicating the mayor in a potential murder conspiracy over some stupid backyard gazebo that probably only costs a few thousand dollars? That feels like a stretch to me."

"It's not a stretch if it's connected to one billion dollars."

Dana's eyes widened. "What?"

David explained how he'd discovered the mayor's son was heading up a lucrative downtown development project with his father's influence. "If the mayor goes down, even on something minor like illegally using city workers' time, it could jeopardize this whole project. A minor slipup could turn into a major problem. And a one-billion-dollar project goes up in smoke."

"You're right," Dana agreed. "It's not a stretch to think someone might take extreme measures to protect that from happening."

David took a moment to let the magnitude of the situation settle on him. He felt like he was suddenly holding a lit stick of dynamite. "Dana, do you still have that friend who works with the Texas Rangers?"

The Texas Rangers were the state's elite law enforcement unit with statewide jurisdiction. They were known for investigating major crimes, unsolved crimes, and public corruption, among other special operations.

She nodded. "Mike Harbers. He's been asking me out for months. Why?"

"If this thing goes as high and as far as we think, we're going to need someone from the outside to help us. This is not a 911 call. Even the police have been coerced and manipulated to hide the truth. We need someone we can trust."

FORTY-SEVEN

David parked his truck in a crowded parking lot right outside Barton Creek Square, which sat high up on a hill overlooking downtown. He got out, pulled his black hoodie up over his head, and hurried inside the Nordstrom department store. Kate had sent him a panicked text message only ten minutes ago. The bald guy with the combat boots had followed her into the mall. She felt like he was becoming bolder, which scared her. She didn't know what to do. David told her to stay put.

Inside the store, David paused, took a long look around him. Nordstrom was busy with shoppers. He spotted no one suspicious at the moment. He walked over to a woman wearing a name tag in the far corner of the first floor, said he was looking for his wife, who was trying on clothes. She led him through an entrance into a hallway of private dressing rooms and knocked on the third door. When it opened, David slipped inside with Kate, who swiftly shut the door behind him. Although there were several clothing items hanging on a hook by the mirror, she wasn't trying anything on at the moment.

"You okay?" David asked.

"No. He's out there right now."

"Where did you see him?"

"I dropped in to return a jacket here. When I turned around, I spotted him a few aisles over, staring at me. I freaked, grabbed some clothes, came in here, and have been waiting on you to get here."

"Did you come here straight from your office?"

She nodded. "He must've followed me."

"What's he wearing?"

"Black jacket, jeans, black boots. And, like, a gray cabbie cap. Did you see him when you walked through the store?"

David shook his head. "But I was hurrying."

Kate swallowed. "Lee was acting *really* weird this afternoon. He'd hardly interact with me."

"They're panicking." David went on to tell her about his discovery of Owen Nelson and the billion-dollar development project.

Kate's face went pale. "What do we do?"

"My friend Dana is reaching out to someone she thinks can help us and protect you from whatever fallout is about to happen. One way or another, we have to bring this to a close. It's become too dangerous for everyone."

She chewed on her bottom lip. "Where do I go from here?"

"I want you to walk out in a minute without me. Instead of going straight back to your car, I want you to go deeper into the mall. Just stroll around for twenty minutes or so, like you're window-shopping, and *then* leave the mall."

"Why?"

"So I can put eyes on this guy. If I spot him, I'll follow him back. And then maybe I can finally ID him. Where are you parked?"

"Right outside the entrance by the kids' shoe department."

"Me, too. What kind of car?"

"Black 4Runner."

"Okay. Drive slowly out of the parking lot. Give me time to get to my truck so that I can follow you closely. And, hopefully, him."

Kate nodded, took a deep breath, and exhaled slowly.

David reached out and touched her arm. "Hey, don't worry. If anything happens, I'll swoop in and tackle this guy, okay? I used to play football, you know."

He gave her a playful grin, trying to get her to relax so she could get through this.

She forced a small smile in return. "My hero. Okay, let's do this already."

Kate opened the door, left the dressing room. David waited a full minute and then also stepped out. He took a peek from the dressing-room hallway into the wide spread of the department store. He didn't spot the bearded guy. He carefully followed a walkway into the busy main mall corridor, hands in pockets, eyes on high alert. Kate was about a hundred feet ahead of him. She was walking slowly, staring into store windows, and doing a good job of not looking terrified. David surveyed the length of the corridor but still couldn't put eyes on the bald, bearded man. He peered up to the second level, seeing if he noticed anyone suspicious staring down over the rails. Where the hell was this guy? He had to still be here somewhere.

David followed at a distance, eyes carefully bouncing from face to face to those all around him. Kate peeled off into a luggage store, began poking through travel bags near the front window. David hugged the opposite wall. He felt a charge race through him when he finally spotted the guy. The bearded man was fifty feet ahead of him, standing off by himself near the front of a mattress store. Black jacket, black boots, gray cap. The man's eyes were firmly set on Kate, who was still inside the luggage store.

David pulled out his phone, carefully raised it in front of him, and snapped several photos of the guy. When the bearded man glanced in his direction, David quickly ducked inside a nearby women's clothing store. A clerk in the store approached and asked David if he needed help, which he politely declined while keeping his eyes out the front window the entire time. Kate stepped out of the luggage store and wandered farther down the corridor. David watched as the bearded man trailed Kate. David then moved all the way across the corridor to monitor the guy from a different angle.

David's cell phone buzzed. A text message from Kate.

You got him?

Yes, go back to your car now.

OK

David watched as Kate turned around and began walking back toward the entrance to Nordstrom. He slipped inside a jewelry shop, held his phone up to his ear as if he were talking to someone as she passed by him. They connected eyes for a brief moment. He hated seeing the fear in hers. It made him want to step out and punch the guy who was following her. When the guy moved past him, David stepped back into the corridor and trailed him.

Kate was walking faster now. She cruised through the aisles of the department store and out the glass doors to the parking lot. The bearded man waited inside the glass doors for a few seconds, watching her return to her car, while David watched him from behind a rack of kids' shoes. Then the guy pushed through the doors and also made his way toward the parking lot. It was David's turn to pause right inside the glass doors. He spotted Kate climbing into her black 4Runner in the middle of the second row. She smartly took her time, allowing everything to play out in a way that gave David a chance to follow.

The man in the gray cap jumped into a green Jeep Wrangler in the third row, quickly backed out. Kate eased out of her parking spot and slowly circled away from the mall. The guy in the Jeep followed. David squinted out the window, took a mental snapshot of the guy's license plate, and then rushed outside and hustled over to his truck. He said a quick prayer as he turned the key. Now was not the time for the truck's old engine to give him any trouble. It roared to life. He backed out, traveled the same circle drive, and caught up with them.

Kate took an exit out of the mall parking lot, did a slow U-turn underneath the MoPac Expressway, then drove the speed limit all the way back into downtown proper. The Jeep Wrangler followed at a safe distance, David trailing the Jeep from even farther back. Finally, Kate pulled into a paid parking lot a block away from the Littlefield Building. Although the guy in the Jeep slowed a bit to watch her get out of the 4Runner, he didn't stop and park. Instead, he turned around and headed south on Congress Avenue.

David did a quick U-turn and followed.

FORTY-EIGHT

David tracked the bearded guy back to a cheap motel on South Congress. The Jeep Wrangler pulled into the parking lot, circled around to the back of the crumbling two-story building, and parked in an outside row. David slowed at the edge of the parking lot as not to be spotted. He counted about a dozen other cars currently parked in the back. The bearded guy got out of his vehicle, took the metal stairs up to the second level, and entered a motel room.

David pulled his truck around until he was close enough to see the number on the outside of the door. Room 237. Then he did a quick U-turn, circled back to the front of the building, and parked right outside the office. A television was on behind the counter in a back room. A guy with curly red hair lounged in a folding chair as David entered, munching on fried chicken from a bucket, his eyes glued to the television.

David rang the bell on the dusty countertop.

"Yep, coming," the guy said with a grunt.

The motel clerk eased his way up to the counter. He was in his twenties and wore a T-shirt that said, *Whiz Kid: Wanna see me whiz?*

"You need a room, bro?" he asked, licking his fingers. "Sixty bucks a night."

"I don't need a room. I need a name."

The guy shifted his eyes. "You a cop?"

David shook his head, pulled two twenty-dollar bills out of his pocket, set them on the countertop. "I got a friend staying in 237. I just need his name, that's all. I'm not going to cause any trouble."

The guy considered it for a long moment, shrugged, and grabbed the money. He stared down at an old computer and began typing. "237?"

David confirmed the room number. The guy laughed.

"What's so funny?" David asked.

"Your friend is famous." He put his palm on the computer monitor, pivoted it so that David could also read the screen: *Tom Cruise*.

"He pay with a credit card?" David asked.

"Nope. Cash. We don't ask a lot of questions around here."

Climbing back into his truck, David drove around to the back of the building again. When he got there, the bearded guy's Jeep was no longer in the same parking spot. He couldn't find it parked anywhere in the lot. It looked like the guy had already left. David cursed. His eyes went back up to the second level and settled on Room 237. Reaching into his glove box, he grabbed a flat-head screwdriver and hustled over to the stairs. When he reached the top, he moved down the outer walkway until he stood in front of 237. There was a window beside the door, but the cheap blinds inside were closed. He took a quick peek but couldn't make out much of anything in the cracks of the blinds. He moved in closer to the door, his ear only inches away, listened but didn't hear anything inside. He put his hand on the doorknob, twisted. Locked. But the knob was *really* loose.

Turning, David examined the parking lot again. No one was currently getting in or out of the other cars. Was he really going to try to do this? Kneeling, he carefully stuck the screwdriver into the crack of the door and began gently jimmying the lock. It didn't take much effort— this wasn't a five-star hotel. The door lock at the jamb easily popped open. David felt his heart racing. He took one last glance behind him, opened the door, and stepped inside. He quickly shut the door behind him and locked it again.

David surveyed the motel room. A disheveled bed. A small circular table with a single chair by the front window. A small dresser against the wall. A tiny bathroom and closet in the back. The table was covered with wadded fast-food wrappers, pizza boxes, and beer cans. The guy was a slob. David quickly sorted through the trash, seeing if anything on the table had a name attached. Nothing. He found a black duffel bag on the tattered tan carpet next to the dresser and began picking through it. Blue jeans, underwear, socks, T-shirts, and a pair of brown cowboy boots. He stuck his hands in the pockets of the jeans and found a pack of cigarettes, some wadded dollar bills, and plenty of loose change. But nothing to identify the guy.

The tiny bathroom was next. A small brown toiletry bag sat on the counter. Next to the bag was deodorant, an electric razor, and a toothbrush and toothpaste. David searched the toiletry bag and *finally* found a name on the outside of a prescription bottle: *Jake Manaford*. The prescription was for Prozac from a clinic in Lake Charles, Louisiana. David pulled out his phone, took a pic of the label. David remembered the text message between Lee Barksdale and Owen Nelson that had pulled Kate into this ordeal in the first place referenced someone by the same name.

Coordinate with Jake and take care of this ASAP.

They had to be one and the same.

Who the hell are you, Jake Manaford?

David was about to do a quick Google search when he heard movement from right outside the motel room door. A punch of panic hit him. Someone was out there. Had Manaford already returned? David's eyes whipped left, right. A mirrored door to the closet was to his immediate right. He tugged it open, slid inside the empty closet, and managed to pull the door just slightly closed when he heard the motel room door swing open. David froze. He still had a three-inch crack in the closet door. He wanted to fully shut it but thought any movement right now could possibly expose him. He inched as far back against the closet wall as possible. He heard keys being dropped on the table near the front, along with what sounded like a sack or something.

David stiffened when Manaford crossed in front of the closet door. The man stepped into the bathroom and relieved himself. David glanced around the dark closet and tried to find some kind of weapon, just in case he had to defend himself. There were a couple of metal hangers but nothing else. Manaford zipped up, moved to the sink, washed his hands. Then he turned and began to examine himself in the full-length mirror on the outside of the closet door. David held his breath, stayed perfectly still. The same guy who probably killed Murphy was only a few inches away from him. If Manaford had any notion to open the closet, David would have to fight his way out of the motel room. He balled his fists, felt sweat beads on his neck.

A sudden knock at the room door startled both him and Manaford. Three quick but firm raps. Manaford stepped away from the closet, walked over to the room door, and pulled it open. David couldn't see who was out there, so he tried to listen closely. He heard a man's voice. It sounded somewhat familiar.

"You the owner of the Jeep Wrangler?"

"Yeah," Manaford grunted. "Why?"

"I'm real sorry, but I accidentally backed up into it with my car. Nothing major, but I didn't want to be the jerk that just drove away. You want to take a look?"

"Yeah, all right."

David heard Manaford grab his keys off the table and leave the room. He knew he had to get out right now, if possible. He opened the closet door, slid out, and rushed over to the front door. He peeked outside and spotted the backs of the two men as they crossed the parking lot over to Manaford's Jeep Wrangler. The other guy wore a black wind-breaker. That's when David put the familiar voice together with the man who'd knocked on the door. Keith Carter—or whatever his real name was. Carter must've been following him and noticed he was caught in a sticky spot. So he swooped in for the rescue. Pulling his black hoodie up over his head, David carefully slipped out of the room and took the outer walkway over to the stairs. He descended to the ground level, kept his eyes on the pavement, and cut through the parking lot behind the guys. David slid up against the motel building, hiding out of the way, and then watched the rest of the encounter between Carter and Manaford.

A gray Ford Taurus was parked directly behind the Jeep Wrangler. David could hear the two men talking about the damage. Manaford said it was no big deal—he didn't have time to mess with insurance and all that. Carter pulled some cash out of his wallet, handed it to Manaford, who climbed into his Jeep. Carter then got into the Taurus, backed out of the way, and headed toward the front of the motel. When he pulled up next to where David was hiding in the shadows, Carter looked straight over at him and gave him a two-finger salute. David held up a finger. But Carter drove off. David thought of running after him but didn't want Manaford to spot him.

Seconds later, Manaford also spun the tires and hit the main street. David knew he was too far away from his truck to catch up with him at this point. He'd have to make do with the information he'd already gotten. He again thought about Carter.

Who the hell was he, really? Was he following David? Or was he following Manaford?

More important, why was he involved in all this?

FORTY-NINE

David drove straight to the hospital to show Rebel the pics of Jake Manaford. Hurrying up to his client's room, he was glad to see two police officers standing guard right outside the door. Billings's TV news spot earlier that afternoon had at least ruffled some feathers and created some movement. Mason had even texted David a string of expletives to let him know how unhappy he was about the story.

Rebel seemed safe—for now. That was all that mattered.

After flashing his ID to the officers, David entered the hospital room. Rebel was wide-awake and watching TV. His client was smiling and laughing at the screen. He seemed really happy to see David.

"Hey, Lawyer! You seen this *Talladega Nights* flick? It's hilarious."

"Yes, I have. How're you feeling?"

"Shoot. Haven't felt this damn good in years."

It was probably all the pain meds. David pulled up a photo on his phone of Manaford inside the mall and held it in front of Rebel. "You recognize this guy?"

Rebel squinted at the screen. The smile immediately disappeared.

"I've seen him somewhere."

"Where, Rebel?"

"I dunno. But I've seen him."

"His name is Jake Manaford. That mean anything to you?"

"Manaford?" Rebel repeated. "Nah, don't know that name. Is he a Russian agent?"

"No," David said, trying to be patient. "Think harder."

"I'm trying," Rebel exclaimed, swallowing and pressing his dry lips together. David heard a nearby machine start to beep more quickly. "I dunno, Lawyer. But I feel like maybe me and this guy had a tussle about something. Just don't know what about."

David wondered if Manaford had been the one to put the jacket and hat on Rebel that night after Kate entered the alley. "Could you have seen him the night Murphy was killed?"

"I don't . . . I can't . . . concentrate."

David turned the TV off. "I really need you to focus. Was this guy there that night?"

Rebel ran a hand through his long hair. He was starting to breathe harder. The machine began beeping even faster, which concerned David. "I'm not sure, Lawyer. But I feel like I've been face-to-face with him. Like maybe I grabbed him by the neck or something."

"Could you have had a physical encounter with him in the alley that night?"

"I don't . . . remember." Rebel was now tugging at his hair with both fists, as if he was getting angry at himself for not being able to pull the information out of his brain.

The machine was really beeping now.

"Rebel, you need to calm down," David urged him.

"Think, you stupid idiot!" Rebel scolded himself. "Think, dammit!"

David wondered if he should call for a nurse.

"Rebel, relax. Take a deep breath. It's okay."

But Rebel couldn't calm himself down. His face was flushed red, and his body was tense. Suddenly, his face went pale, his eyes rolled back into his head, and he went perfectly still. The beeping turned into a solid stream.

"Rebel!" David gasped. "Help!"

Two nurses rushed into the room, shoving David out of the way.

"His blood pressure is dropping," one nurse said. "He's crashing."

"Sir, I need you to clear the room!" the other nurse ordered David.

"Rebel, relax!" David begged his client.

"Sir! Clear the room right now!"

David slid outside as a doctor and two more nurses raced inside to work on Rebel. He watched through the partially closed doorway, his own heart beating rapidly. After all this, was Rebel going to die from sudden cardiac arrest? Was it David's fault? Had he pushed Rebel too far for his current condition to handle? The doctor had warned him about the irregular heartbeat and the possibility of ventricular fibrillation. When David heard the shock of a defibrillator inside the room, he cursed, then immediately began praying for his client—and his friend. It could not end this way.

"He going to die?" one of the officers standing nearby asked David.

David looked over at him. "No!"

"Good. I don't want to get into trouble over this."

David glared a hole into the officer, turned away, paced in a tight circle in the hallway. More shocking noises and commotion inside. Then everything went eerily quiet in the hospital room. David swallowed. Either Rebel had finally stabilized. Or his friend was dead.

The doctor stepped out into the hallway.

"Doc?" David said.

"He's going to be okay," the doctor reassured him.

David slowly exhaled, relaxed his hands. He hadn't even realized he'd had both fists squeezed into tight balls. "Thank you."

"But he needs to stay calm," the doctor instructed. "He's highly vulnerable right now. Whatever just happened in there with you can't happen again. Do you understand?"

"I understand."

FIFTY

David found Thomas and Doc huddled around the entry table in the front room of their office suite when he arrived from the hospital. David had texted Thomas about Manaford right after he'd left the motel earlier, so his partner and Doc had been busy researching everything they could find on the guy. Thomas was writing things on the whiteboard while Doc was sitting at the table with his fingers pecking away at a laptop. Jake Manaford's name was written at the very top of the board. There was a short list of bullet points below his name. David dropped heavily into a chair, rubbed his face, exhausted from what had just happened. The doctor said Rebel was going to be out for a while. Which was fine. David had no intention of even bringing up the case with Rebel anymore. It was too risky.

"How's our client?" Thomas asked.

"I damn near killed him," David said, shaking his head.

Both Thomas and Doc stopped what they were doing to look over at David.

"What happened?" Doc asked.

"I showed him a photo of Manaford. He *definitely* recognized the guy, but he couldn't remember much else—only that he thought he'd had a face-to-face encounter. Then he got himself so worked up about not being able to remember that he went into cardiac arrest. They had to get the damn paddles out to bring him back. For a minute or so, I really thought we were going lose him."

"Sheesh," Doc said.

"He's okay now?" Thomas asked.

"Yes. But he needs to take it easy."

The mutt, Sandy, rushed out of the back room upon hearing David's voice. He scooped the dog up and began petting him. "Your old man just scared the hell out of me," he told Sandy. Then he began studying the whiteboard. "Get me caught up."

Thomas began pointing. "Manaford was born in Louisiana in '85. Found an address for him in Lake Charles. Google Maps showed it to be a run-down apartment building. Looks like he did a short stint in the navy. Manaford has a criminal record. He's been arrested several times for petty crimes like theft, disorderly conduct, and vandalism. In and out of jail several times, from what I can tell. He doesn't do social media—at least under his given name. No Facebook, Twitter, or Instagram accounts. Doc found something tying him to an auto shop in Lake Charles. I called the shop, and a guy there said Manaford did oil changes for them for a while but then got fired for showing up drunk too many times. That's about as far as we've gotten."

"So he's a lowlife nobody?" David asked.

"That appears to be the case," Thomas agreed.

"We can't find a connection yet," Doc chimed in. "But Larue just texted me. He said he showed a photo of Manaford to Skater, who confirmed this was the same guy who tried to bribe him the other day—and then threatened his life if he said anything."

"Maybe he's just a hired gun," Thomas suggested.

David shook his head. "No, we're missing *something*. If he was only a hired gun, I think Manaford would've come into town, handled his business, and then left. But he has continued to stay intricately involved in this whole thing."

"We'll keep digging," Thomas said.

"Okay, thanks." David set the dog on the floor. "I've got to go talk to a drummer to see if I can finally find Mia Martinez."

FIFTY-ONE

David entered the Parish music venue on Sixth Street. He took the stairs up to the second level and could hear a band playing in fits and starts as they did a sound check. The Dragon Parrots were set to perform later tonight, so David hoped to catch them early in order to talk to the drummer, Scott Harrison. He found a group of guys on the small stage that looked just like the band members on the website with their long, grungy hair and all-black wardrobe.

David stood in the back of the room and watched. The band guys kept giving out instructions over live microphones while the two guys in the sound booth made various adjustments. Then they would jam out at full volume for a couple of minutes at a time as they made their way through a set list. David studied the drummer. It was definitely Harrison. His black hair was the longest in the band.

David scanned the rest of the near-empty room, seeing if he could spot Mia anywhere nearby. There were a couple of young girls over on the side, chatting away, but neither of them was Mia. One was blonde, the other brunette. The sound check took another twenty minutes before the band finally finished, and a set of new guys strolled onto the stage and began setting up.

David stepped over before Harrison could go anywhere.

"Scott, right?" he said, standing next to the drummer.

Harrison was busy packing up some of his drum gear.

He looked up. "Yeah, what's up?"

David just came right out with it. "My name's David Adams. I'm an attorney. I need to find Mia ASAP."

David studied Harrison closely. The guy seemed startled by the request, his eyes widening for a second, before he tried to act casual and play it off.

"Mia?" he said, zipping up a small bag.

"Yeah, Mia Martinez. Your girlfriend."

He shrugged. "I don't know where she is right now. Why're you looking for her?"

"I'm trying to save her life, Scott. So don't play games with me."

Harrison paused, pitched his head. He didn't act puzzled, which led David to believe the guy already knew something serious was going on with Mia. For a second, Harrison didn't even seem to know how to respond to David.

"I don't . . . What do you mean . . . ?" Harrison stuttered.

"Her life is in danger. Where is she?"

"Look, man, I don't know what the hell is going on, okay? So leave me alone."

Frustrated, David took a business card from his pocket, held it out for the guy. "If you care at all about Mia, you'll get this to her right away. Tell her to call me. I may be the only chance she has to make it out of this alive."

The guy hesitantly took the card.

FIFTY-TWO

When he returned to the office, David was surprised to find that Dana had joined Thomas and Doc in the front room. David could tell something big was going on. Upon his entry, each of them looked up with the widest eyes—like they'd seen a damn ghost or something.

"What's going on?" David asked.

Dana handed him her phone. "Take a look at this."

David took the phone. She had a video ready to play. "What is this?"

"City camera. The night of Murphy's death. Tell me if you recognize someone."

David pressed "Play." It was a security camera view pointed up a sidewalk. The street looked familiar. People were casually strolling. The date-and-time stamp at the top of the video was approximately the same moment that Murphy had been gunned down in the alley. A few seconds into the video, a small collection of people suddenly scrambled out of an alley, like they were running away from something. Most of them looked like homeless vagrants. The fourth man caught his attention. He was bald, bearded, and wore a white T-shirt and jeans. David cursed. Jake Manaford. He rewound the video and watched it again. Manaford's face was as clear as day in the glow of a lamppost while rushing out of the alley. He quickly sprinted out of view of the camera. Two seconds later, another familiar figure appeared from the alley. Rebel. His client looked frantic. Rebel glanced left, right, and then hurried down the sidewalk.

"Where did you get this?" David asked Dana.

"I made some threats, threw my weight around. I'm probably going to get fired."

"No wonder they didn't want to give this to us," Thomas stated.

"Manaford had to have put the jacket and hat on Rebel," Doc said. "Nobody was out that night in nothing but a T-shirt. It was cold as hell."

"Has Mason seen this yet?" David asked Dana.

"Hell no!" she snapped. "I don't trust *anyone* over there right now."

"Okay, good."

"There's more," Dana said. "After you texted me his name and photo earlier, I began digging around into his criminal background. I found a name that looked familiar to me from one of the times Manaford was bailed out of jail several years back. A woman named Margaret Jackson posted for him."

"Who is Margaret Jackson?" David asked.

"Manaford's mother. She changed her name to Margaret Nelson when she remarried."

"You're kidding?" David said. "The mayor's wife?"

Dana nodded. "Manaford is the mayor's stepson."

"A family affair." David shook his head. "Did you talk to your Ranger friend?"

"Yes. Mike's going to his boss. He wants us to come in right now."

"You trust him?"

"I do. We've got to get Manaford off the streets before he kills someone else."

"Agreed. Let me reach out to Kate."

But before he could even text Kate, she texted him. He pulled his phone out, read her message, and felt full-blown panic race through him. "I've got to go!"

FIFTY-THREE

David drove like a madman down Rainey Street and slammed on his brakes right outside of a casual bar with an outside patio called Clive. He peered left, right, searching for Kate. Her text said when she'd come home to her downtown high-rise apartment tonight, she'd found it completely ransacked. So she'd immediately rushed out of the building and was hiding in the back of the bar across the street.

Kate stepped out of the bar seconds later, jumped into the passenger seat, and ducked down really low. David could see that she was shaking.

"You okay?" David asked.

"Please, just drive," she begged him.

David pulled off the curb, circled a side street.

"Was someone still inside?" he asked.

"I heard something. But I was too shocked and scared to stick around to find out. If someone was in my apartment doing this, it means they know about me, David."

"You're right. It's time to pull the plug."

"Where are we going?"

"To meet Dana and her Texas Ranger friend."

Kate rubbed her face in her hands. "I just want this to be over with already."

"Me, too. Believe me."

"Still no luck with Mia?"

"No, her boyfriend wouldn't give her up. But we can't afford to wait around any longer. Not with what we found out about your stalker today."

David quickly explained what had happened at the motel earlier, along with the discovery of Manaford's real identity and his familial connection to the mayor.

Kate sank even deeper into the seat. "So who is this Carter guy?"

"I don't have a clue—and that makes me really nervous."

David turned onto Cesar Chavez, eased into evening traffic. His phone buzzed in his pocket. He pulled it out, stared at the random number. He'd been answering all calls since he'd given his business card to Scott Harrison earlier, each time hoping it might be Mia, only to be disappointed when it was someone else.

"This is David."

At first, there was no response. Then a quiet voice.

"This is Mia Martinez."

David swerved his truck into a nearby parking lot, stopped, put his phone on speaker. "Are you okay, Mia?"

"I've been in hiding for almost a week. What do you think?"

"I want to help you."

"How? You're just an attorney."

"I know people, okay? I'm actually in my truck right now, taking another witness to get her under police protection. I can do that for you, too."

David heard a click. Had she hung up?

"Mia?" he said.

A long pause but no dial tone. She was still on the line. David had to keep her talking. She was likely the final piece of the puzzle. Plus, he could not allow another innocent person to be taken out because of this crime. Too much blood had already been spilled.

"Mia, please talk to me. You're not safe."

"I can't. I'm sorry—"

Kate spoke up. "Mia, you can trust David. I promise."

"Who are you?" Mia asked.

"Someone who's scared, just like you."

"You know who is behind all of this?"

"We think we do," David answered. "But you can probably help us fill in the gaps."

"They killed my brother."

"I know," David said. "I'm sorry. They killed my friend, too."

"Luke Murphy was your friend?"

"Yes. They also tried to kill my client last night."

"I saw that on the news today."

"Then you know you're in serious danger out there by yourself."

"I don't know what to do."

"Tell us where you are," Kate said. "We'll come straight there."

Mia was silent again. David could hear her breathing heavily. He looked over at Kate, who sat there with wide eyes. They both knew this was the moment of truth.

"Mia?" Kate said.

"AMLI Downtown," Mia said. "Apartment 414."

She hung up. David put the truck into drive and punched the gas pedal.

FIFTY-FOUR

The AMLI Downtown was a traditional seven-story apartment building located on Second Street in the heart of the restaurant-and-shopping district. David swerved his truck in and out of traffic and arrived in under two minutes. He pulled into an open spot along the curb, and they jumped out. He could tell Kate felt the exact same thing he did—this was *the* pivotal moment. David didn't even bother paying the parking meter. He couldn't waste a single second. They raced around the corner of the apartment complex and found a metal-gated entrance to the building between two busy street-level restaurants. They bypassed an elevator and instead took the outside stairs. David bounded up two and three steps at a time with Kate nipping at his heels.

David found Apartment 414 midway down the hallway. He paused for a moment, took a breath, peered up and down the hallway, and then gently knocked. He could feel the adrenaline pumping through him. Mia didn't answer right away, which made him nervous. Could she have gotten cold feet and bolted within the few minutes it took them to get there? He was about to knock again when the door cracked open, and he found a woman in her early twenties peeking out.

At first, he didn't think it was Mia—even though she had the same brown eyes as in her Facebook pictures. All her online photos showed her with medium-length black hair, but this girl had very short hair that was dyed blonde. She must have cut and colored her hair to hide better.

"Mia?" David asked.

She hesitantly nodded. He could see the fear behind her eyes.

"I'm David. This is Kate."

Mia looked back and forth between them.

"Can we come in?" Kate asked.

Mia nodded again, pulled the door open, and allowed them to enter. She quickly shut the door behind them and secured the two locks. Mia wore blue jeans, black tennis shoes, and a burnt-orange UT sweatshirt. She looked nervous as hell, her every movement a bit shaky. David did a quick scan of the one-bedroom apartment. It was decorated to the nines with nice furniture and what looked like expensive artwork on every wall.

"Are you here alone?" David asked her.

"Yes. This is my boyfriend's sister's apartment. She's an art dealer who is in Europe this month. Scott got the key and has been letting me hide out here."

Kate stepped closer to Mia. "Are you physically harmed in any way?"

"Other than being a complete mental case, I'm fine." She looked over at David. "How did you know to come looking for me?"

"Why don't we sit for a moment, so we can talk?"

Mia moved to a big chair in the living room, while David and Kate sat next to each other on a leather sofa. Kate took a moment to tell Mia about the texted photo of her brother that she had seen on Barksdale's phone and the trail it had led her down with Murphy, his death in the alley, and then Kate's reaching out to David for help. David followed that up by telling Mia about visiting her mother, going to her apartment, and finding out through one of her classmates about her drummer boyfriend.

Mia's eyes became wet. "Not talking to my mom has been the hardest thing this past week. I keep getting her texts and voice mails. But I can't respond to her, because I'm trying to protect her. All of this is my fault. I could've stopped this from ever happening. But I didn't—and now my brother is dead."

"What happened?" David said.

Mia sighed. "Eddie had been having a hard time lately. His girlfriend left him with their two kids and took off back to Mexico a few months ago. So he moved in with our mother recently to get some help. My mother has also been struggling because my father passed away suddenly last year. He was their only real source of income, so she's way behind on the mortgage. We've been trying to figure out what to do as a family so that she doesn't lose the house."

"I'm sorry to hear that," Kate said to Mia.

"Yeah, it's been stressful, especially on Eddie. He felt like he was supposed to take care of the whole family now that Dad was gone. Well, Eddie was hanging out at my apartment two weeks ago when he mentioned he was working on a project in Mayor Nelson's own backyard—his crew was building some kind of gazebo next to the pool. He thought it was kind of cool being at the mayor's house and seeing him come and go. But I told him what he was doing was actually illegal. He wasn't allowed to do personal work for a city official while being paid by the city. I had just read about a case up in New York where a mayor got busted for doing the same thing. He pled guilty to conspiracy charges and is now spending five years in prison. Well, this gave Eddie the dumb idea that maybe we could use the situation somehow to help Mom save her house. At first, I told Eddie he was crazy. But then I also felt so desperate. My mother was so grief-stricken over my dad. I feared if she were to lose the house, too—where they'd lived for over thirty years—it just might crush her whole spirit."

"So you went along with it?" David asked.

Mia nodded. "I was so stupid. I should've stopped him."

"What did Eddie do?"

"The next day, he took some pictures on his phone of them working at the mayor's house. Then he left a typed note I had written on the mayor's back door that said we had information that could be damaging to the mayor and wanted to speak with him. Eddie had purchased a burner phone to take the photos and use with all of this, and he left the phone number. Within hours, Eddie got a phone call, but it wasn't the mayor. It was some other guy demanding to know what this was all about. Telling my brother it was illegal to threaten the mayor like this, and he could go to jail."

"Did he identify himself?" Kate asked.

Mia shook her head. "No, but Eddie didn't back down. He texted the photos to the guy and said he wanted twenty-five thousand dollars in cash. Eddie wanted to ask for a lot more money, but I told him that we needed to play it more conservative. If we went too high, it would probably just cause us bigger problems. But if we asked for something more moderate, we just might get paid off to go away."

"What happened next?" David asked.

"The guy said he'd call Eddie back. We waited two days and didn't hear *anything*, although Eddie and his crew immediately got removed from the gazebo job. I figured they weren't taking us seriously, and it was all pretty much over. Which was fine with me. I was already regretting the whole thing. But then Eddie got the call. The guy said he had our money, and they made plans to do an exchange that night. Eddie chose a place he knew well. I demanded to go with him, even though my brother was pissed about it. I told him we were in this together. I waited in the car while Eddie met a guy across the parking lot. The guy handed him an envelope, and everything seemed to be going smooth. I thought we were just going to drive out of there with the money we needed to save my mom's house. But then this guy suddenly pulls a gun out and . . ." Her voice began to crack. "He shot my brother right in the head. Eddie just fell straight backward and never moved."

Kate got up from the sofa, sat right next to Mia in the chair, and wrapped her arm around her. Mia eased into her like she desperately needed the comforting.

"Did the guy see you?" David asked Mia.

"I couldn't be sure. We were parked across the lot. But he glanced over toward the car, so I immediately jumped out and just took off running."

David pulled his phone out. He knelt in front of Mia and showed her the photos of Jake Manaford. "Is this the guy?"

Mia's eyes flashed open. "Yes! That's the guy!"

David felt a new shot of adrenaline. Mia had directly connected Manaford.

"His name is Jake Manaford," Kate explained. "He's the mayor's stepson."

Mia shook her head. "I never thought something like this would happen."

Kate consoled her. "We're dealing with some really sinister people here."

"What did you do next?" David asked.

"That night, I hid out at my boyfriend's garage apartment. He was on the road with his band. And I watched the news unfold about my brother's death—only the story quickly got twisted into some kind of supposed drug deal gone bad. They were saying they found drugs in my brother's car, which I knew was a complete lie. That made me afraid to call the police and tell them the truth. I drove to my mom's house first thing the next morning, just so we could cry about Eddie together. But I never told her *anything* about what really happened. I tried to go back to class, but I just walked around paranoid as hell the next two days. I couldn't sleep. I couldn't focus. Then this guy from the DA's office comes looking for me in between classes."

"Luke Murphy?" David said.

Mia nodded. "He said he was investigating the circumstances behind my brother's death. At first, I wasn't sure I could trust him. But then he suggested that he didn't believe my brother had been killed over a drug deal. I was so desperate, I told him what really happened and gave him the photos Eddie had used. He promised to help and said he would get back to me the next day. But then he was shot dead that night. When I came back to my apartment the next morning after staying at my boyfriend's again, I found it completely destroyed. Someone had been inside. So I took off and have been hiding out ever since, praying this whole thing will somehow just go away. I even cut off all my hair and dyed it in hopes that I couldn't be recognized. I just want this to all be over."

"Me, too, Mia," Kate said. "With your help, it will be."

"I'll do whatever I have to do to end this."

"Then you need to come with us right now," David said.

"I'm ready."

FIFTY-FIVE

David was on the phone with Dana, coordinating how to meet, with Kate and Mia right on his heels, when he turned the corner of the apartment building hallway toward the stairwell and heard a loud *thump*. Then he felt something whiz right past his left ear and explode against the wall behind him. He jerked back, unsure what had just happened. Mia gasped. Kate grabbed David by the arm from behind. Then he heard a second loud *thump* followed by another wall explosion only inches away from them. For a split second, David felt like he was having an out-of-body experience. Was someone shooting at them? Searching frantically, David spotted Manaford coming up the metal stairs toward them at full speed with his gun in his right hand. David cursed. Manaford must've somehow followed them from Kate's apartment building and simply waited to take them out. David couldn't allow that to happen. Not when he'd promised the two women with him that he'd keep them safe. Not when they were so close to solving this whole conspiracy and finally bringing justice to the situation.

Spinning around, David yelled, "Go! Run!" and pushed Kate and Mia back in the opposite direction. David heard another gunshot, and a bullet hit the corner of the hallway wall just as he slipped out of reach on the other side.

"Is there another stairway?" David yelled ahead to Mia.

"Yes! Follow me!"

They sprinted down the hallway past Apartment 414 again and darted around the next corner. A woman opened the door of an apartment just ahead of them and looked out with a scrunched-up face. David yelled for her to go back inside and call the police. She quickly slammed the door shut. Without slowing down, David glanced behind him. Manaford spun around the same hallway corner and was still coming on hard. David turned back and moved to the center of the hallway in an effort to shield Kate and Mia from any potential gunfire. His whole body tightened, as if he could somehow weather the impact of a bullet. They turned down another hallway. Ahead of him, Mia located the second set of metal stairs, and they quickly descended.

David could hear Manaford's boots pounding on the metal stairs above them. David knew he had to protect Kate and Mia from this guy. Manaford was shooting at them out in the open. They couldn't just keep running. He just needed to find the right moment. They reached the second level. The *thump* of a gunshot rang out from above them and ricocheted off the metal stairs at their feet. Mia screamed, but David yelled for them to keep moving.

When they reached the street level, David spotted a metal door leading to the underground parking garage. Racing past Kate and Mia, he shoved open the door and held it for them both to get through as swiftly as possible.

He then grabbed Kate's arm, pulled her back, handed her his truck keys. "I'll meet you at the truck. If I'm not there in five minutes, go without me."

"David!" Kate exclaimed.

"Just go!"

She followed his instructions and hurried with Mia into the bowels of the parking garage. David could hear Manaford approaching on the other side of the door. He scooted back into the corner behind the garage door and did a countdown in his mind. Three, two, one. The garage door burst open, and Manaford appeared. The man paused for a moment, gun in hand, searching for them. David took that moment to sprint toward him from behind. With all the force he could muster in a few steps, David drove his right shoulder into the guy's midsection, like a linebacker sacking a quarterback, and tackled the big guy. Manaford dropped forward, his face hitting flat against the hard floor of the garage. The gun flipped out of his hand and skidded into the shadows of the garage.

David quickly pushed himself up. With Manaford momentarily dazed, David kicked him several times as hard as he could in the ribs. Manaford let out painful grunts and balled himself up on the floor, gasping for breath. David then kicked the man square in the face, snapping the guy's head way back. Manaford lay perfectly still on the concrete.

Standing there, David felt his chest rise and fall rapidly. He could now hear multiple sirens right outside the apartment building, followed by car doors opening and slamming, and then lots of yelling. The police had arrived. David took another glance at Manaford. The guy wasn't moving. He looked down for the count. When David heard what sounded like police coming into the hallway just beyond the parking garage door, he spun around and sprinted out of the garage. He would let them take over from here. He wasn't interested in trying to explain the situation to beat cops. He had to get back to Kate and Mia.

It was time to help them get their lives back. It was time to exonerate his client. It was time to bring the real men behind Murphy's death to justice.

It was finally time to end this.

FIFTY-SIX

They huddled inside the main conference room at the local news station. David wanted this story broadcast as wide and loud as possible—to cast the brightest spotlight—so that no one in power could run and hide in the shadows. David had a bag of ice pressed against one cheek, which had begun to swell from his violent collision with Manaford. He stood at the window of the conference room and watched the city street two floors below. Kate and Mia sat in two leather chairs around the conference table, where the young TV reporter, Theodore Billings, had his notepad out and was grilling them with questions. He could tell the kid was in heaven right now and was probably already dreaming of journalism awards. A woman named Wendy Dobson, the station's news director, along with Emily Harris, the assistant news director, were both in the room. So was a man in a suit named Eric Juliard, the station's lead attorney. They all carefully monitored the conversation between Billings and Kate and Mia. There were a lot of wide eyes and shaking of heads as both Kate and Mia unveiled what would likely be the biggest news story the local station had ever produced.

David was leaning in closer to the window when a black Suburban pulled up in front of the TV station. Dana got out of the front passenger seat. Four men all wearing cowboy hats and boots, white dress shirts with ties, and khaki pants also climbed out of the vehicle. Together, the group marched toward the entrance of the building.

David stepped away from the window, walked out of the conference room, and met Dana and the four Texas Rangers in the hallway outside the newsroom.

Dana introduced Lieutenant Mike Harbers and the other three guys. Harbers was a tall clean-cut man in his thirties with a square jaw. He looked like he should probably be on the official poster for the Rangers. David quickly shook hands.

"Glad to see you guys," David said.

"You okay?" Mike asked him, eyeballing his swollen cheek.

"I'll live. You pick up Jake Manaford?"

David had immediately called Dana to give her the news about Manaford.

"Police have him in custody," Mike confirmed. "We'll grab him shortly. From everything Dana has shared with us, we're about to have a big mess to clean up."

"Yeah, I think we're going to need more than just the four of you."

Harbers smiled. "Don't worry, David. I have about twenty of my buddies waiting for my instructions. Let's get started."

"Follow me."

David led them inside the conference room, where he introduced them to all the other parties. David could tell by the relieved looks on Kate's and Mia's faces they were glad to see law enforcement figures they felt like they could finally trust. Wendy said they were only a few minutes away from beginning to shoot video. Billings was going over the details again with both Mia and Kate, making sure he got all his facts straight. Kate met David's eyes from across the room. He pitched his head to the side, as if asking if she was good. She pressed her lips together and nodded.

Dana sidled up next to him. "Are you really okay?"

"I am now that you're here with your pals."

"Believe me, they are the right ones for this investigation. It's going to be chaos. I just hope I still have a job after all of this blows up."

"You can always come work for me."

She smiled. "I just may have to take you up on that one day. You know, you really scared the hell out of me back there at the apartment building."

David pitched his head slightly. "How?"

"We were on the phone together, remember?" she explained. "You must've put your phone in your pocket without hanging up when you took off running. I was unable to make out much of what was going on, but I could tell you were in big trouble. I've never felt more relieved than when you finally called me back. I've already lost Murphy. I can't lose you, too, David."

"I'm not going anywhere." David leaned in and gave her a quick peck on the cheek. "Anyone over at the DA's office know what's going on over here at the station right now?"

"Nope. They're all going to find out the same time as the rest of Austin."

David smiled. "Can you take care of things here, Dana?"

"Where are you going?"

"I need to go see my client."

FIFTY-SEVEN

David entered Rebel's quiet hospital room and found his client doing much better than he had been earlier that day, when he'd given everyone a good scare. Rebel seemed calm and collected, and all the color was back in his face.

David walked up to his bedside. "How're you doing, buddy?"

Rebel held up a hand, as if to stop him. "I don't want to see no more pictures, Lawyer. Doc says my heart can't take the excitement right now. I need a couple more days for my body to get stronger, so they can put that damn heart gadget in me."

David smiled. "Don't worry. I don't have pictures. But I do have good news."

Rebel looked up at him. "Well, don't just stand there. Start spittin'."

"By tomorrow morning, I'm expecting all charges to be dropped against you. When you finally leave this hospital, you'll be walking out a free man again."

Rebel's eyes narrowed. "You messing with me, Lawyer? I already told you my heart can't take it."

"I'm dead serious. It's over."

David watched as his client's eyes teared up. Seeing the raw emotional release in his friend's weathered face made his own eyes begin to water. He swallowed, tried to hold back the emotions. But he couldn't help himself. He would've never guessed the incredible bond he would forge with this man when they'd first met in that private jail room a few days ago. Just like with Benny, David had entered a situation thinking he was there to rescue the vulnerable only to realize the vulnerable were rescuing him right back. In that moment, he'd never felt more sure of his place as an attorney.

Soon, they both had tears dropping.

"Stop crying," Rebel told him.

"I'm not crying. You're crying."

Rebel chuckled, wiped a tear away with the top of his hand. "Look at us. Two grown men bawling like babies. What a pathetic sight. Aw, hell, get down here, Lawyer, and give me a hug already."

David leaned over him, and they squeezed each other good.

"I'll never forget this," Rebel said to him.

"I'll never forget you," David replied. "But I'm keeping your dog."

They shared another good laugh.

"So how'd you do it, Lawyer? How'd you get me free?"

"Turn on the news and I'll show you."

FIFTY-EIGHT

One week later

David shuffled a few boxes around on the dusty floor of his near-empty office. Most everything was already packed. There were stacks of boxes in the entry room. Movers were scheduled to come tomorrow to get all the furniture. For now, everything the firm owned was being put into a storage unit until they could find another office suite that fit their needs—which meant it had to be dirt cheap. The law firm of Gray & Adams, LLP was basically bankrupt. Now that Rebel's case was over, David had promised Thomas he'd roll up his sleeves and begin building his paying client list. He would get them back on their feet again soon—somehow. He'd already received several calls inquiring about his legal services in the aftermath of Rebel's dramatic acquittal last week.

Rebel still had a few more days in the hospital before finally being released. He said he might go back to California. David offered to drive him there himself.

The investigation had led to several immediate arrests. Jake Manaford had been charged with first-degree murder in the deaths of Eduardo Martinez and Luke Murphy. Lee Barksdale and Owen Nelson were charged with conspiring to commit murder. Of course, the arrest of Mayor Gregory Nelson on obstruction charges was the biggest spectacle. David had spoken with Lieutenant Harbers from the Texas Rangers, who told him that while it looked like the mayor was not necessarily guilty of murder, the man *was* guilty of having a wicked, power-hungry son. Owen Nelson had apparently taken matters into his own hands when he found out his father was being blackmailed. He'd pulled his buddy lawyer, Barksdale, into it, along with his criminal stepbrother. When his father discovered all this in the aftermath of Rebel's arrest, the mayor began to scramble to protect both his position in office and his sons. DA Jeff Jordan had also walked out in handcuffs for his role in abusing his power to help protect the mayor. In the end, they would all end up serving time in prison. As it turned out, Neil Mason was guilty only of being a pompous ass and following orders from a corrupt boss.

David taped up another box. He stood, walked to his office window, where he could see the sun setting on the day. He was going to miss this view out over Congress Avenue. Then he heard a familiar voice come from his office door.

"You need a hand?"

David turned, saw Keith Carter standing there. He hadn't seen the man since that day with the incident at the motel. He'd been beginning to wonder if he'd ever see him again.

"You've already given me several hands. Who the hell are you?"

"I have many names, David."

"Well, one of them is not Keith Carter. That's for sure."

Carter gave him a tight grin. "No, I'm afraid not."

"So who are you?"

"Who I am is not important. What's important is that I need your help."

"Help with what?"

"I need to talk to Mr. North."

David wrinkled his nose. "So . . . go talk to him. He's not in custody anymore."

"It's not that easy. I don't think Mr. North will talk to me without you there."

"Why?"

Carter shut the office door behind him, stepped even farther into the room. "The things I need to discuss with him involve sensitive intelligence information and are a big part of what put Mr. North on edge. I think your being there might help him relax."

David's mouth parted. "Wait . . . *intelligence information*?"

"David, we've been searching for Mr. North for five years after discovering that he'd developed a couple of key relationships with important foreign contacts during his time with us. Believe me, he's been a very difficult individual to track down—probably because we trained him to operate in the shadows."

"Hold up a second," David said, his mind spinning. "Are you telling me the CIA thing is real? He didn't make this all up?"

"I'm sure you have a lot of questions. Most of which I'm afraid I can't answer."

David put both hands on his head. He couldn't believe it. The CIA really had been hunting Rebel for the last five years?

He looked over at Carter. "You found him when he was arrested?"

"Correct."

"If you're the CIA, why didn't you just go get him from jail? Don't you guys do that kind of thing? Swoop in and take people away in the middle of the night?"

"You have to understand something, David. What I'm a part of doesn't officially exist. So we're in no position to play with bureaucracy here. Not to mention this case has been a spectacle from the beginning."

"So you've just been waiting around, hoping I'd get him out?"

"I think I've done more than that. And now that I've helped you, I would like you to return the favor."

David suddenly felt very protective. "Look, I'm not letting you take him back to this dragon's lair place he always talks about."

"That place no longer exists. I only want to talk to him."

David was on the fence. Carter had definitely helped him get Rebel out of jail. But would Rebel consider it a betrayal if David then brought the CIA to him? Still, if Carter was telling the truth—and he only wanted to talk with his client—it might finally free Rebel from the chains of paranoia that had completely wrecked his life.

"I have to be there for every conversation," David insisted.

"I'd prefer it."

David spent another hour packing up boxes. He was still reeling from his exchange with Carter earlier. They'd come to an agreement that David would begin a conversation with Rebel tomorrow morning and see if he'd be willing to have the proposed discussion with Carter. David wasn't sure what to expect. But he knew he'd be there for Rebel every step of the way.

Finishing up with the boxes, David hauled them downstairs and out onto the front sidewalk, where he began loading them into the back of his truck.

"Sir, are you David Adams?"

David turned around and found a guy in his twenties standing there wearing a blue sport coat. "Yep, that's me."

"My name is Max Headley. I deliver for US Couriers. I have a certified package for you."

"A package from whom?"

Max read the envelope. "The estate of Nicholas North."

"Who?"

Max shrugged. "Arkansas address. I just deliver, sir."

Nicholas North? Was that the name of Rebel's dead uncle? He showed the courier the required ID, signed for the document, received the sealed envelope. After the guy left, he tore it open and stared down at a check written out to Gray & Adams, LLP for $200,000. His mouth dropped wide-open. Below the check was a note: *Two peas in a pod, you and me.* David stared at the dollar amount again and couldn't believe his eyes. Rebel had casually mentioned his uncle had left him a little money—but this was not just a *little* money.

Thomas bounded down the building steps with two boxes in his arms. "Don't just stand there. These boxes aren't going to pack themselves, you know."

David met Thomas with the widest grin.

"What are you so happy about?" Thomas asked.

"I think we're going to be okay."

"Why? Stop messing around."

David handed his partner the check.

Thomas looked up at him with bulging eyes. "Is this for real? Rebel?"

David nodded. "A courier just handed it to me."

"I—I don't even know what to say."

"I think you could say this is a *very* big day for our firm."

Thomas matched his grin. Soon they were both smiling like idiots.

"I'm sure glad I told you to take this case," Thomas said.

"Ha! Well, you were right."

"I've got to go call Lori with the news!"

David watched as his partner raced back inside the building.

Standing there, David stared up into the sky and couldn't stop smiling. Somewhere up there, he had a feeling that Benny was smiling right back.

AUTHOR'S NOTE

For the past fourteen years, I've had the life-changing opportunity to build genuine relationships with so many homeless individuals through my work with a nonprofit called Mobile Loaves & Fishes and the Community First! Village—a fifty-one-acre master-planned community in Austin that provides affordable, permanent housing and a supportive community for those coming out of chronic homelessness. I write about these experiences and how they helped inspire *An Equal Justice* and *An Unequal Defense* on my website at www.chadzunker.com. I hope you'll check it out. The impact my street friends have had on me far outweighs anything I could ever offer them in return. Near the end of the book, David says he entered the situation with Rebel thinking he was there to rescue the vulnerable, only to realize the vulnerable were rescuing him right back.

That's also my story—told over and over again.

ABOUT THE AUTHOR

Chad Zunker is the author of the David Adams legal thriller *An Equal Justice*, as well as *The Tracker*, *Shadow Shepherd*, and *Hunt the Lion* in his Sam Callahan series. He studied journalism at the University of Texas, where he was also on the football team. Chad has worked for some of the country's most powerful law firms and has also invented baby products that are sold all over the world. He lives in Austin with his wife, Katie, and their three daughters and is hard at work on his next novel. For more information, visit www.chadzunker.com.